AF527575

BUILDING A FUTURE READY INDIA

VISION PLAN & STRATEGY FOR TECHNICAL EDUCATION DURING AMRIT KAAL

Enhancing the Role of Technical Education for **VIKSIT BHARAT**

Prof. (Dr.) T G Sitharam
Chairman,
All India Council for Technical Education (AICTE)

KHANNA PUBLISHING HOUSE
Delhi (Bharat)

Dear Readers,

To prevent the piracy, this book is secured with HIGH SECURITY HOLOGRAM on the front title cover. In case you don't find the hologram on the front cover title, please write us to at contact@khannabooks.com or whatsapp us at +91-99109 09320 and avail special gift voucher for yourself.

Specimen of Hologram on front Cover title: 

Moreover, there is a SPECIAL DISCOUNT COUPON for you with EVERY HOLOGRAM.

How to avail this SPECIAL DISCOUNT:

Step 1: Scratch the hologram
Step 2: Under the scratch area, your "coupon code" is available
Step 3: Logon to www.khannabooks.com
Step 4: Use your "coupon code" in the shopping cart and get your copy at a special discount
Step 5: Enjoy your reading!

Thanks,
Khanna Publishing House

ISBN: 978-93-5538-611-3

To view complete list of books, please scan the QR Code:

BUILDING A FUTURE READY INDIA

by Prof. T .G. Sitharam, Chairman
All India Council for Technical Education

First Edition: 2025

Published by:
Khanna Book Publishing Co. (P) Ltd.
CIN: U22110DL1998PTC095547

Address: 4C/4344, Ansari Road, Daryaganj, New Delhi-110002 (Bharat).

Phone: 011-2324 44 47 -48, 4321 5684
Customer Care: +91-99109 09320
Email: contact@khannabooks.com
Visit us at: www.khannabooks.com

Printed in Bharat.

Copyright © Reserved with Author

No part of this publication may be reproduced, stored in a retrieval system or transmitted, in any form or by any means, electronic, mechanical, photocopying, recording or otherwise without prior permission of the author.

This book is sold subject to the condition that it shall not, by way of trade, be lent, re-sold, hired out or otherwise disposed of without the publisher's consent, in any form of binding or cover other than that in which it is published.

डॉ. सुभाष सरकार
Dr. SUBHAS SARKAR

सत्यमेव जयते

राज्य मंत्री
शिक्षा मंत्रालय
भारत सरकार
MINISTER OF STATE
FOR EDUCATION
GOVERNMENT OF INDIA

Foreword

It brings me great joy to present this remarkable technical masterpiece, showcasing the latest advancements in its field. In today's rapidly evolving world, technological innovation is pivotal for progress, and this book serves as a testament to the relentless pursuit of excellence in this domain.

As we navigate the intersection of innovation and progress, envisioning the future of technical education becomes both an aspiration and a necessity. "Vision for Technical Education by 2047" offers a profound exploration of the aspirations, challenges, and transformative possibilities that lie ahead.

As a nation, India has long recognized the crucial role of education in shaping our country's destiny. In this visionary work, the authors meticulously crafted a roadmap for technical education up to 2047, grounded in current trends, societal needs, and technological advancements.

The book titled 'Building a Future Ready India: Vision Plan and Strategy for Technical Education during Amrit Kaal,' focuses on enhancing technical education's role for a developed India, a dream shared by 1.42 billion people.

I commend the author for their foresight, dedication, and commitment to shaping a brighter future through education. His vision is not just aspirational but also a call for action to all the stakeholders—educators, policymakers, industry leaders, and students—to collectively strive for a future where technical education empowers individuals and propels nations forward.

I extend my heartfelt congratulations to the authors on this remarkable achievement, and I urge every reader to explore the wealth of knowledge within these pages. May this book inspire innovation, ignite creativity, and foster a passion for technological excellence.

(Dr. Subhas Sarkar)

Office : Room No. 104-A, 'C' Wing, Shastri Bhawan, New Delhi-110 001, Tel. : +91-11-23384327, 23381302, Fax No. : +91-11-23782052
E-mail : mosedu-ss@gov.in

भारतीय राष्ट्रीय अभियांत्रिकी अकादमी
Indian National Academy of Engineering
Ground Floor, Block-II, Technology Bhavan, New Mehrauli Road, New Delhi- 110016
भूतल, ब्लॉक–II, प्रौद्योगिकी भवन, न्यू महरौली रोड, नई दिल्ली–110016
दूरभाष/Phone: (91) 011–26582475, ई–मेल/Email: inaehq@inae.in, वैबसाईट/Website: www.inae.in

प्रोफ़ेसर इंद्रनील मान्ना/ Professor Indranil Manna
FNAE, FTWAS, FNA, FNASc, FASc, MAPAM, FIE(I), FIIM, FEMSI, FAScT, PRS, DSc(hc) PhD

Vice-Chancellor,
Birla Institute of Technology (BIT) Mesra
Ranchi, Jharkhand, 835215, India
Tel.: 0651-2275402, Fax 0651- 2275401
Email: imanna@metal.iitkgp.ac.in
im_kgp@yahoo.co.in

अध्यक्ष/ President

Foreword

In the journey of a nation's progress, education stands as the cornerstone upon which aspirations are built, and dreams take flight. "Building a Future-Ready India: Vision, Plan, and Strategy for Technical Education by 2047" is not just a book but a blueprint for shaping the destiny of a burgeoning India.

As we set our sights on 2047, the centenary year of our nation's independence, it becomes imperative to chart a course that propels us towards a future teeming with possibilities. Technical education, with its ability to fuel innovation, empower minds, and drive economic growth, becomes the fulcrum upon which our aspirations pivot. Education, especially in the engineering and technology domain, is not just about imparting knowledge; it's about fostering a culture of innovation, critical thinking, and adaptability. This book serves as a catalyst for conversations and actions that will shape the very fabric of engineering education in the coming decades.

With the world evolving at an unprecedented pace, a proactive and forward-thinking approach become important to navigate these dynamic shifts. The wisdom shared in this book will serve as a compass, navigating the complexities of the technological landscape. This book is meticulously crafted to envision a robust framework for engineering education—a blueprint that transcends barriers, embraces inclusivity, and fosters an ecosystem of innovation and entrepreneurship.

This book serves as a guiding beacon to equip the youth with the skills and knowledge necessary to thrive in an increasingly complex world. It calls upon educators, policymakers, and visionaries to collaborate in sculpting an educational landscape that empowers generations and ensures India's prominence on the global stage.

I commend the author for his dedication in presenting this roadmap, inviting us all to envision a future where technical education becomes the catalyst for a prosperous and inclusive India. I am confident that this book will serve as an enduring resource, guiding and inspiring generations of researchers, students, and practitioners in their pursuit of excellence.

May this book ignite the flames of innovation, inspire collaboration, and serve as a guiding compass as we collectively endeavour to build a future-ready India by 2047.

I convey my best wishes for the widespread dissemination and adoption of the book amongst the concerned stakeholders and success in meeting the objectives at the National Level.

Indranil Manna

Prof. Indranil Manna

President
Indian National Academy of Engineering (INAE)

"I commit all proceeds of this book towards setting up AI Labs or Scholarships through Anuvandini Foundation, section 8 company of AICTE."

— T.G. Sitharam

"May there always be light."

ABOUT THE AUTHOR

Prof. T. G. Sitharam
Chairman, AICTE, India

Prof. T G Sitharam owes and owns an everlasting debt of gratitude to Lord Rama. He regards it as a profound blessing and a testament to his life's work that his design now rests at the feet of Lord Rama in the Ram Janmabhoomi, serving as the foundation of the sacred temple. He is deeply humbled and eternally grateful for the divine privilege of contributing to this monumental endeavor. He is a Visionary Leader in Technical Education and Civil Engineering. He is currently serving as the Chairman of the All India Council of Technical Education (AICTE) since December 2022, and spearheading efforts to modernize technical education in India. He has profoundly influenced technical education shaping the future of India's academic and engineering landscape. His leadership emphasizes innovation, employability, inclusivity, and alignment with global standards. Sitharam who studied in Kannada medium during his school education, at AICTE he has championed technical education in regional languages, fostering inclusivity for students from diverse linguistic backgrounds. His involvement with yoga and meditation connects with his commitment to holistic education and well-being. He has been an advocate for integrating traditional Indian knowledge systems with modern technical education, promoting a balanced approach to personal and professional development.

During his long service to Indian Institute of Science, Bengaluru; he created and nurtured CiSTUP (Center for infrastructure, sustainable transport and urban planning) at IISc Bengaluru and state of the art laboratory for geotechnical earthquake engineering at Civil Engineering Department of IISc, Bengaluru to pursue his research work in the geotechnical earthquake engineering field. Previously, as Director of the Indian Institute of Technology (IIT) Guwahati (2019–2022), Prof. Sitharam demonstrated exemplary administrative acumen and contributed significantly to institutional growth. During his tenure, IIT Guwahati established five new schools and five multidisciplinary academic centers, improved its global standing, and notably ranked 37th in the QS World Ranking for citations per faculty. He also oversaw the establishment of a medical school and a multispecialty hospital at the institute, in collaboration with the Government of Assam. Prof. Sitharam's academic journey began with a Bachelor's in Civil Engineering from the University of Mysore. He pursued a Master's at the Indian Institute of Science (IISc), Bangalore, in 1986 and earned a Ph.D. from the University of Waterloo, Canada, in 1991. Further, he was University of Texas at Austin pursuing his post doctoral work for 2 years. Over the years, he has held prestigious academic positions at renowned international institutions, including the University of Waterloo (Canada), the University of Texas at Austin (USA), the University of Hong Kong, the University of Wollongong (Australia), and Dalhousie University (Canada).

His leadership roles span institutions such as IIT Guwahati, NERIST, CSIR-CBRI, and the Central Institute of Technology Kokrajhar. Prof. Sitharam is globally recognized for his expertise in civil infrastructure, geotechnical engineering, seismic microzonation,7 soil dynamics, and geotechnical earthquake engineering. With over 35 years of experience, he has authored approximately 500 technical papers and 20 books, Guided over 40 Ph.D. students, Filed five patents and initiated two startups. His Google Scholar H-index of 58, I-10 index of 175, and over 11,030 citations. His work has earned him a place among the top 2% of the world's most-cited scientists (Stanford University, 2020–2024). He is a fellow of Indian National Academy of Engineering (INAE); American Society of Civil Engineers (ASCE); Institution of Civil Engineers (ICE), UK. In October 2024, the Institution of Engineers (India) honored him as an Eminent Engineering Personality at the Thirty-Ninth National Convention of Civil Engineers in Kochi. Prof. Sitharam is a recipient of Sir M. Visvesvaraya Lifetime Achievement Award (2023) and Sir C.V. Raman State Award for Young Scientists, Govt of Karnataka, for the year 2002 in recognition and appreciation of exceptional contributions to Engineering Sciences in Karnataka, and many other awards and accolades he received during his entire career, which reinforce him as a distinguished scientist, engineer, and educator, dedicated to advancing knowledge and solving critical challenges in engineering and beyond.

GRATITUDE

- Prof. T. G. Sitharam dedicates this book foremost to Goddess Saraswati's limitless blessings and the transformative power of education.
- To All India Council of Technical Education (AICTE) and the entire officers, staff who have influenced the author to pen this book.
- **To my beloved father:** Your wisdom, values, and unwavering belief in my potential have been the guiding light of my life. Your encouragement and sacrifices laid the foundation for everything I have achieved. Thank you for inspiring me to dream big and work hard to achieve those dreams.
- **To my dearest mother:** Your unconditional love, resilience, and constant prayers have been my greatest strength. Your nurturing spirit and support have been the source of my confidence and courage. I owe my journey to the selfless love and sacrifices you have made.
- **To my loving wife Dr. M V Anuradha:** Your continuous engagement, patience, understanding, and support have been my anchor through every challenge and milestone. Your unwavering faith in me and support has been a constant source of strength and motivation. I am deeply grateful for your presence in my life and the balance you bring.
- **To Arundhati and Aditya Bhargava:** My wonderful children you are my pride and joy, and the inspiration that keeps me striving for excellence. Your curiosity, enthusiasm, and love inspire me with the importance of building a better future for all the young children that i have been chosen by God to serve. I hope my journey serves as an example of dedication and perseverance for you.
- **To my mother-in-law:** Thank you for your kindness and unwavering support. You have not only raised our children but have also become a cherished part of our life. Your warmth and love inspire all of us every day, and I am so grateful for the support to Aru, Aditya and all of us. We owe you an everlasting debt of love and appreciation.
- To my esteemed colleagues at IISc, IIT Guwahati, AICTE, eminent technocrats, my teachers, friends and students that allowed me to touch their lives.

PREFACE

In the rapidly evolving landscape of technical education, the year 2047 stands as a pivotal juncture for India. This book delves into the transformational journey of technical education over the past few decades, offer insights on vision, plan and strategy for technical education in India, harness the potential of technical education in nation building and foresight into the innovations, challenges, and possibilities that have defined this dynamic era.

The significance of technical education has soared to unprecedented heights in the last few years. India envisions a holistic Technical Education System that produces globally competitive skilled technical professionals. With the rise of artificial intelligence, quantum computing and sustainable engineering solutions, a paradigm shift is necessary to impart skill based knowledge and prepare future generations.

This book is an attempt to understand the key elements of Technical Education which includes 'Quality Education, Leveraging Technology, Integration of Skill in Curriculum, Promotion of R&D, Innovation in Pedagogy, Industry-Academia Collaboration etc.

Drawing upon the collective wisdom of visionaries, educators, and pioneers in the field, this book endeavors to illuminate the transformative forces shaping technical education. It seeks to inspire educators, students, policymakers, and innovators alike to envision and co-create a future where learning is agile, inclusive, and empowers individuals to thrive in an ever-evolving world.

TABLE OF
CONTENTS

1. EXECUTIVE SUMMARY

As we approach the dawn of a new era, it becomes increasingly imperative to realize the potential of Technical Education in shaping a better tomorrow. In the context of India, a nation of diversity and complexity, it is vital that we harness the full potential of Technical Education in nation-building. In light of this, a comprehensive blue print of the Vision, Plan, and Strategy for Technical Education by 2047 is essential.

The National Education Policy 2020 and the All India Council for Technical Education (AICTE) have laid the foundation for the realization of this vision. India's position as the educational and knowledge capital of the world is further strengthened by the emphasis on Technical Education. Make in India, the flagship initiative of the government, is also a testament to the importance of Technical Education in India's growth story. However, the realization of this vision is not without its challenges. It requires concerted efforts and multi-sectoral partnerships to overcome the obstacles in the path of Technical Education. The need to build a culture of research and innovation, to address the challenges of rural Technical Education, and to cater to the needs of differently-abled students are some of the challenges that need to be addressed.

Moreover, the importance of financial aid and scholarships in promoting Technical Education, the need for soft skills, critical thinking, problem- solving, lifelong learning, and experiential learning in enhancing the employability of Technical Education graduates, and the challenges of online and hybrid Technical Education are all critical issues that need to be addressed.

VISION

By 2047, India envisions a holistic and agile Technical Education system that produces globally competitive skilled technical professionals who contribute to innovation & research, and promote commitment to lifelong learning and ethical inclusive education to shape our nation as the top leader of global education.

MISSION

- Provide access to quality education to all students, regardless of their social or economic background.
- Develop the technical hands on exposure and soft skills of students to enhance employability and enabling them to apply their knowledge in the real world and contribute effectively in their professional careers.
- Enable curriculum and pedagogical approaches that foster a culture of lifelong learning and problem-solving.
- Incorporating mentoring system to ensure holistic development of students, fostering a supportive and engaging learning environment that goes beyond structured classroom instructions.
- Promote innovation & entrepreneurship and enable research and product development in areas of emerging technologies that can garner benefits to society by adhering to SDG's.

PLAN

The plan for Technical Education in India shall aim to provide access to quality education to all students, regardless of their geographical location or socio-economic background. The plan shall focus on enhancing the infrastructure and facilities of technical institutions and promote industry-academia collaborations to provide practical training to students. The plan shall also aim to develop the curriculum and course content in line with industry requirements and promote research and development in emerging areas of technology.

STRATEGY

The strategy for Technical Education in India shall aim to create a sustainable ecosystem that can provide quality education to students. The strategy will focus on leveraging technology to enhance the delivery of education and create a flexible and adaptive learning environment. The strategy shall also aim to develop partnerships with international institutions and promote global collaboration to provide a diverse and inclusive education to students.

ANALYSIS

To evaluate the success of this vision, it is essential to have effective monitoring and evaluation mechanisms in place. This will require the implementation of a comprehensive plan that focuses on the vision, plan, and strategy for Technical Education by 2047.

Technical Education is the key to unlock India's potential and building a future-ready nation. The realization of this vision requires the collaboration of all stakeholders and a sustained effort towards the development of Technical Education in India. The journey towards 2047 will be challenging, but with a clear vision, plan, and strategy, we can achieve a better tomorrow.

The Vision, Plan, and Strategy for Technical Education by 2047, is a path-breaking comprehensive blueprint of Technical Education contributing to Hon'ble Prime Minister Shri Narendra Modi's clarion call of Viksit Bharat by 2047. With the enhancement of Technical Education, India can play a vital role in nation-building and become a hub for innovation, entrepreneurship, and economic development. However, to unlock India's potential through technical education, important initiatives needs to be implemented along with addressing the forthcoming challenges.

KEY INITIATIVES

There are several key initiatives that can be undertaken to implement the vision, plan, and strategy for Technical Education in India. Some of these include:

- Enhancing the quality and accessibility of technical institutions.
- Promoting industry-academia collaborations to provide practical training to students.
- Developing a flexible and adaptive learning environment that leverages technology.
- Developing the curriculum and course content in line with industry requirements by involving relevant domain industry experts by giving equal emphasis to theory and practice.
- Creating a learning mode culture based on applied and practical based experiential learning.
- Promoting research and development in emerging areas of technology.
- Developing partnerships with international institutions to provide a diverse and inclusive education to students.
- Promoting industry professionals to engage as Professor of Practice in higher educational institutions.
- Promoting diversity and inclusion in technical education by formulating adaptive learning environments.
- Encouraging innovation, entrepreneurship and start up ecosystem among students.
- Providing opportunities for continuous professional development and upskilling.
- Fostering a culture of research and innovation.
- Developing sustainable models for Technical Education in India.

The details of AICTE schemes are available at www.aicte-india.org

CHALLENGES

There are several challenges that need to be addressed to implement the vision, plan, and strategy for Technical Education in India. Some of these include:

- Lack of infrastructure and resources in technical institutions.
- Shortage of qualified faculty and trainers.
- Disconnect between industry and academia.
- Lack of access to practical training and exposure to emerging technologies.
- Slow adoption of technology in the delivery of education.
- Insufficient investment in research and development.
- Limited opportunities for international exposure and collaboration.
- Inadequate funding for Technical Education.
- Lack of benchmark performance indicators or metrics to assess the success of efforts to bridge the employability gap.
- Limited focus on soft skills, language development and entrepreneurship development.
- Lack of cross-disciplinary collaboration between academic departments and industry sectors to address complex real-world problems.
- Lack of applied internship opportunities.
- Insufficient monitoring and evaluation of the quality of Technical Education.

2. IMPORTANCE OF TECHNICAL EDUCATION

Education serves as the quintessential cornerstone of an individual's life, and it's been entrenched in the cultural ethos of India since time immemorial, serving as the harbinger of success. With the advent of industrialization and the digital revolution, there has been a paradigm shift towards Technical Education in India, and it's become increasingly pertinent to fathom its significance. This vision document delves deep into the importance of Technical Education in India, the government's initiatives, and the National Education Policy 2020, culminating in a comprehensive understanding of the subject.

Technical Education, spanning across a broad spectrum of subjects such as engineering, technology, architecture, management, and many more, has taken a pivotal role in the development of any nation, and India is no exception. It facilitates students with practical skills and applied knowledge, aiding them in their professional lives, while simultaneously contributing to the country's infrastructure development and economic growth. India, with a burgeoning young population, presents a unique opportunity to harness its potential and spur the country's growth. Technical Education serves as one of the key catalysts in attaining this goal. Proper education and training, when availed, enable the youth to contribute substantially to the country's economic development.

The field of Technical Education has become increasingly important in India as the country seeks to position itself as a global leader in innovation and technology. With the introduction of the National Education Policy 2020 and the initiatives of the All India Council for Technical Education (AICTE), there is a renewed focus on the development of Technical Education in India. One of the primary goals of Technical Education is to produce skilled professionals who can contribute to the development of various sectors of the economy, including manufacturing, infrastructure, and services. As India seeks to become a manufacturing hub through initiatives such as Make in India, the importance of Technical Education cannot be overstated.

In order to achieve this vision, India needs a workforce with the necessary technical skills and knowledge.

Moreover, Technical Education also plays a vital role in positioning India as an educational capital of the world. With the rise of digital technology, online education, and global connectivity, India has the opportunity to become a leading provider of Technical Education to students from all over the world. The quality of Technical Education in India has improved significantly in recent years, with many institutions offering world-class programs and facilities.

In addition to positioning India as an educational capital, Technical Education also has the potential to establish India as a knowledge capital of the world. India has a rich history of scientific and technological innovation, from the invention of zero to the development of the world's first satellite. Through Technical Education, India can continue to produce a steady stream of innovators and entrepreneurs who can drive technological progress and advance the country's standing in the global knowledge economy.

The Indian Government, cognizant of the importance of Technical Education, has implemented a plethora of initiatives. This include establishment of renowned Engineering Colleges and Institutions.

- **First Four Engineering Colleges of India:** The first engineering college was established in India a century before the Independence. Thomason College of Civil Engineering was established in 1847, later converted to the University of Roorkee in 1948. In July 1854, College of Engineering in Pune was established, followed by Calcutta Civil Engineering College in West Bengal in 1856. College of Engineering, Guindy was founded in 1794 as Asia's oldest technical institution and was affiliated to the University of Madras in 1858.
- **IISc & IISER:** The Indian Institute of Science was established in 1911 in Bangalore. The Government of India has also established seven Indian Institutes of Science Education and Research (IISERs). These institutes are located in Berhampur, Bhopal, Mohali, Pune, Kolkata, Thiruvananthapuram and Tirupati. These are the country's premier institutes for academic research into both fundamental and interdisciplinary sciences.
- **IITs:** The establishment of Indian Institutes of Technology (IITs) stands out as one of the notable efforts, given their reputation for providing world- class Technical Education and attracting students globally. Presently, 23 IITs are operational, and the Government plans to inaugurate more such institutes in the future.
- **NITs & IIITs:** In addition to IITs, the Government has also founded National Institutes of Technology (NITs) and Indian Institutes of Information Technology (IIITs) to promote Technical Education. These institutions provide quality Technical Education to students, nourishing the country's technical workforce.

Furthermore, the Government has introduced various schemes to foster Technical Education. The Pradhan Mantri Kaushal Vikas Yojana (PMKVY) stands as a prime example, aiming to provide skill training to the youth. Financial assistance is furnished to students wishing to pursue Technical Education under this scheme.

Image showcasing 23 IITs across India

The National Education Policy 2020 (NEP) is a revolutionary policy document that intends to revamp the Indian education system entirely. The policy envisions a new education system that is flexible, multidisciplinary, and holistic. It prioritizes providing quality education to all students and preparing them for the future. NEP 2020 recognizes the importance of Technical Education in the country and emphasizes its promotion. It proposes establishing a National Research Foundation **(ANRF)** to boost research in the country, including Technical Education. Moreover, the policy proposes setting up new technical universities and colleges to meet the surging demand for Technical Education.

According to the All India Survey on Higher Education (AISHE) 2019-20, **India has a total of 10,988 technical institutes. The enrolment stands at 42.98 lakh students**, out of which 23.77 lakh are male students and 19.21 lakh are female students. The majority of students pursuing Technical Education are enrolled in engineering courses.

Technical Education is indispensable for India's development, providing students with practical skills and knowledge, rendering them employable, and contributing to the nation's economic growth. The Indian Government's initiatives and the NEP 2020 aim to promote Technical Education, providing ample opportunities for the youth to prosper and augment the country's growth. The implementation of these initiatives requires a comprehensive strategy that includes effective monitoring and evaluation. It is important to regularly assess the success of the vision, plan, and strategy for Technical Education in India to ensure that the country is on track to achieve its goals. This requires the involvement of all stakeholders, including policymakers, educators, employers, and students.

National Education Policy -2020 provides a blueprint for transitioning the Indian Technical Education to global standards by focusing on the following parameters:

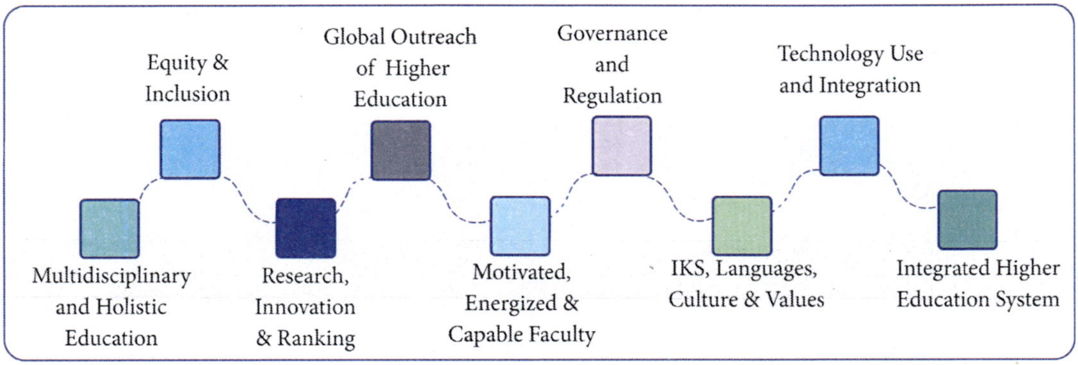

3. OVERVIEW OF GROWTH OF TECHNICAL EDUCATION IN INDIA

India's history of education dates back to ancient times, when the transmission of knowledge occurring through the Guru-Shishya tradition. However, the focus of education during that era was primarily centred on religious, astrology, science and spiritual learning. In the aftermath of British colonialism, India embraced modern Technical Education. This vision document aims to delve into the intricacies of the historical evolution of Technical Education in India, including pertinent government initiatives, and a comprehensive analysis of statistical data.

The origins of Technical Education in India can be traced back to the establishment of Thomason College of Engineering in Roorkee in 1847, which primarily aimed to train civil engineers for the construction of canals, railways, bridges, and other infrastructure projects. The founding of Thomason College is considered as the precursor to the Technical Education revolution in India.

In the aftermath of India's independence in 1947, the government recognized the criticality of Technical Education in promoting industrial growth and development. Consequently, in 1951, the first Indian Institute of Technology (IIT) was established in Kharagpur, West Bengal.

The institution offered courses in engineering and technology, and it became a cornerstone for Technical Education in India. Since then, several IITs have been established throughout the country, bolstering Technical Education significantly.

In an effort to promote Technical Education in India, the government of India has taken various initiatives. The All India Council for Technical Education (AICTE) was constituted in 1945 as an advisory body and became regulator in 1987. The AICTE was established with a view to the proper planning and co- ordinated development of the technical education system throughout the country, the promotion of qualitative improvement of such education in relation to planned quantitative growth and the regulation and proper maintenance of norms and standards in the technical education system.

According to the All India Survey on Higher Education (AISHE), the majority of students enrolled in technical institutes are pursuing engineering courses.

The AISHE data suggests that the demand for Technical Education is growing, emphasizing the criticality of promoting and supporting Technical Education.

The evolution of Technical Education in India is rich in history and complexity. The government has taken several initiatives to promote Technical Education in India, empowering the youth with the skills and knowledge required to navigate the 21st century economy.

The statistical data highlights the increasing demand for Technical Education among the youth, further emphasizing the need for continued support and promotion of Technical Education in India. In the year 2022-23, the number of UG seats approved by AICTE in various disciplines of core engineering has seen good enrolments on an average. The number of approved intake and enrollment in undergraduate programme of Engineering as follows:

Engineering UG Degree Seats Intake and Enrolment for Year 2022-23

Engineering disciplines	Seats intake	Enrolment
Civil	136273	79056
Electronics and Communication	164380	136115
Electrical	47147	34503
Mechanical	170364	103045
Computer Science	390968	376048

ABOUT AICTE

Initial Set-up

All India Council for Technical Education (AICTE) was set up in November 1945 as a national-level apex advisory body to conduct a survey on the facilities available for technical education and to promote development in the country in a coordinated and integrated manner. And to ensure the same, as stipulated in the National Policy of Education (1986), AICTE was vested with:

- Statutory authority for planning, formulation, and maintenance of norms & standards
- Quality assurance through accreditation
- Funding in priority areas, monitoring, and evaluation
- Maintaining parity of certification & awards
- The management of technical education in the country

4. VISION FOR TECHNICAL EDUCATION IN INDIA BY 2047

India's Technical Education system has come a long way since its inception. The government's initiatives and efforts have enabled the country to produce some of the most talented and skilled technical professionals in the world. However, AICTE is putting its plan to make India a global leader in Technical Education. This vision document aims to define a vision for Technical Education in India by 2047, outlining strategies, implementation plans, and government initiatives to achieve this vision.

Vision: By 2047, India envisions a holistic and agile Technical Education system that produces globally competitive skilled technical professionals who contribute to innovation & research, and promote commitment to lifelong learning and ethical inclusive education to shape our nation as the top leader of global education. The vision of Viksit Bharat aims to develop the quality of entrepreneurship amongst the youth to make them job givers rather than job seekers.

Mission Statement:

- Provide access to quality education to all students, regardless of their social or economic background.
- Develop the technical hands-on exposure and soft skills of students to enhance employability competence and enabling them to apply their knowledge in the real world and contribute effectively in their professional careers.
- Enable curriculum and pedagogical approaches that foster a culture of lifelong learning and problem-solving.
- Promote innovation, startup eco system & entrepreneurship and enable research and product development in areas of emerging technologies that can garner benefits to society.
- Establish India as the global hub for skilled technical talent and as a global leader in innovation, research and development.

Strategy Plan:

The following strategies will be employed to achieve the vision for Technical Education in India by 2047:

Promoting Innovation and Entrepreneurship:

- The Indian government aims to create a culture of innovation and entrepreneurship among students. The government will encourage the establishment of innovation and entrepreneurship centers in all Technical Education institutions.
- Incubations and accelerators within higher educational technical institutions will nurture inventions and startups. These centers will provide an eco-system mentorship, funding, and resources to students who want to start their own businesses or pursue innovative projects.

Industry-Academia Collaboration: To promote practical learning, the government will encourage industry-academia collaborations. Technical Education institutions will collaborate with industry experts to design and deliver courses that are relevant to industry needs. Industry experts will also provide training, mentorship, and job opportunities to students. Core industry experts will be invited to orient faculties about latest trends and applications in their respective domain areas.

Upgrading Curriculum: To keep pace with the rapidly changing technological landscape, the government will regularly update the Technical Education curriculum. The curriculum will include emerging technologies such as artificial intelligence, machine learning, and the internet of things.

Promoting Research and Development: The government will encourage Technical Education institutions to conduct applied and fast track research and development activities to cater the needs of industry. The government will provide funding and resources to institutions that undertake research projects that can contribute to the country's technological advancement.

Implementation Plan:

To achieve the vision for Technical Education in India by 2047, the following implementation plan will be adopted:

- Development of India as a hub for world class talent in Technical and Management Education.
- Attract and retain the best engineering from a more inclusive and dynamic pool of Indian talent from other countries.
- **Establishing New Institutions:** The government will establish new Technical Education institutions across the country. The new institutions will be established in underdeveloped regions to promote equity in access to Technical Education with an emphasize on Research and Innovation.
- **Building Infrastructure:** The government will invest in building world- class infrastructure in Technical Education institutions. This will include modern classrooms, laboratories, and research facilities.
- **Faculty Development:** The government will provide funding and resources to institutions to develop the hands on technical as well as mentoring skills of their faculty. The government will encourage institutions to hire industry experts as visiting faculty to provide practical learning experiences to teachers and researchers.
- **Promoting Digital Learning:** The government will promote the use of technology in education. Technical Education institutions will be encouraged to adopt digital learning platforms to provide quality education to students across the country.
- Promote innovation, startups and entrepreneurship to create a pool of job creators from Engineering and Management students.

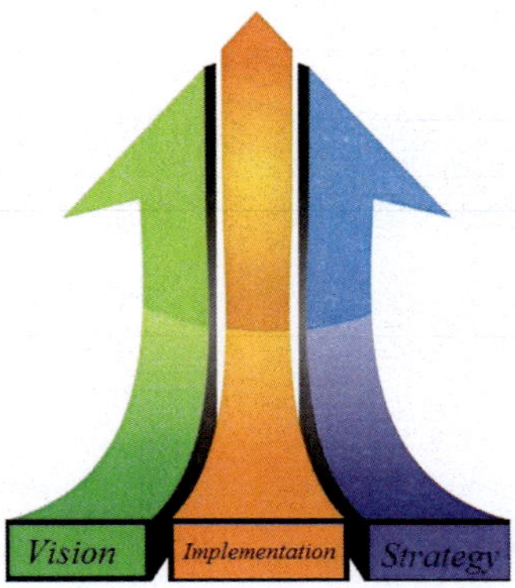

5. CHALLENGES FACED IN TECHNICAL EDUCATION & HOW TO OVERCOME THEM

Technical Education in India has been grappling with numerous challenges that have put a strain on its growth and development. These hurdles span across inadequate infrastructure, scarcity of funds, antiquated curriculum, and insufficient faculty training. In this discourse, we shall scrutinize the challenges facing Technical Education in India and propose compelling strategies and implementation plans that can surmount them.

Challenges

- **Inadequate Infrastructure:** Technical Education institutions in India are beleaguered by a dearth of state-of-the-art infrastructure. Many institutions lack modern classrooms, laboratories, and research facilities, impeding their ability to furnish quality education.
- **Lack of Funding:** Technical Education institutions in India are grappling with a deficit of funding. Many institutions are struggling to finance research and development activities, which impede their capacity to remain current with the rapidly evolving technological landscape.
- **Outdated Curriculum:** Technical Education curriculum in India is often antiquated and fails to align with the latest technological advancements. This impedes the acquisition of relevant skills and knowledge by students and widens industry – academia gap.
- **Inadequate Faculty Training:** Technical Education faculty members in India often lack the necessary expertise and training to deliver top-notch education. This impairs the capacity of institutions to dispense quality education to students.
- **Lack of Innovation:** The culture of innovation and startups in Indian Institutions is often seen neglected, thereby creating a hindrance for students to develop innovative skills.

Strategies

To surmount these challenges, the following strategies will be implemented:

- **Investment in Infrastructure:** The government should prioritize investing in world-class infrastructure in Technical Education institutions. This will encompass state-of-the-art classrooms, laboratories, and research facilities. The government should also allocate funds for the upkeep of the existing infrastructure.
- **Increased Funding:** The government should enhance funding for Technical Education institutions. The government should allocate funds for research and development activities, equipment, and infrastructure development.

- **Curriculum Upgradation:** The government should periodically update the Technical Education curriculum to reflect the latest technological advancements. The curriculum should incorporate emerging technologies such as artificial intelligence, machine learning, IoT and other relevant and upcoming technologies by taking expert views of domain and industry professionals.
- **Faculty Development:** The government should provide resources and funds to institutions to enhance the skills of their faculty. The government should urge institutions to engage industry experts as visiting faculty to provide practical learning experiences to students.

Implementation Plan

To achieve the vision for Technical Education in India by 2047, the following implementation plan will be adopted:

- Development of India as a hub for world class talent in Technical and Management Education.
- Attract and retain the best engineering from a more inclusive and dynamic pool of Indian talent from other countries.
- **Establishing New Institutions:** The government will establish new Technical Education institutions across the country. The new institutions will be established in underdeveloped regions to promote equity in access to Technical Education with an emphasize on Research and Innovation.
- **Building Infrastructure:** The government will invest in building world- class infrastructure in Technical Education institutions. This will include modern classrooms, laboratories, and research facilities.
- **Faculty Development:** The government will provide funding and resources to institutions to develop the hands on technical as well as mentoring skills of their faculty. The government will encourage institutions to hire industry experts as visiting faculty to provide practical learning experiences to teachers and researchers.

- **Promoting Digital Learning:** The government will promote the use of technology in education. Technical Education institutions will be encouraged to adopt digital learning platforms to provide quality education to students across the country.
- Promote innovation, startups and entrepreneurship to create a pool of job creators from Engineering and Management students.

NATIONAL EDUCATION POLICY 2020

The National Education Policy 2020 seeks to revolutionize the country's education system. The policy underscores the significance of Technical Education and aims to provide equitable access to quality Technical Education to all students. The policy proposes amongst other recommendation the following actionable goals pertaining to Technical Education in India:

Integration of Vocational Education: The policy suggests the integration of vocational education into mainstream education. This will provide students with opportunities to acquire practical skills and experience.

Establishment of Innovation and Entrepreneurship Hubs: The policy proposes the establishment of innovation and entrepreneurship hubs in Technical Education institutions. These hubs will provide mentorship, funding, and resources to students who want to start their businesses or pursue innovative projects.

Emphasis on Research and Development: The policy emphasizes the importance of research and development in Technical Education. The policy proposes the establishment of research and development cells in Technical Education institutions

AICTE in line with NEP has brought changes in the newly launched Approval Process Handbook 2024-27 with a vision to make the process of approval seamless and light with tight regulations. Also, AICTE introduced education programmes for working professionals to upgrade their academic qualification at all levels.

6. IMPACT OF TECHNICAL EDUCATION ON ACHIEVEMENT OF SDG GOALS

Technical Education has become an increasingly critical component of India's development strategy in recent times. The sustainable development goals (SDGs), which serve as a roadmap for the country to achieve sustainable economic growth, social inclusion, and environmental sustainability, have emphasized the significance of Technical Education in advancing these goals. In this vision document, we shall delve into the profound impact of Technical Education on sustainable development goals in India.

The sustainable development goals, which were adopted by the United Nations in 2015, are a set of 17 inter linked SDG goals. These goals encompass the social, economic, and environmental dimensions of sustainable development and are designed to be integrated and mutually reinforcing, emphasizing the need to achieve sustainable development in a holistic and integrated manner. Among these goals are no poverty, zero hunger, good health and well-being, quality education, gender equality, clean water and sanitation, affordable and clean energy, decent work and economic growth, industry, innovation and infrastructure, reduced inequalities, sustainable cities and communities, responsible consumption and production, climate action, life below water, life on land, peace, justice and strong institutions, and partnerships for the goals.

Technical Education has a significant impact on several sustainable development goals. For instance, Technical Education provides quality education to students, equipping them with the skills and knowledge required to succeed in the 21st century. This, in turn, is essential for achieving sustainable development goals such as good health and well-being, decent work and economic growth, and reduced inequalities.

Furthermore, Technical Education plays a vital role in advancing industry, innovation, and infrastructure in India by equipping students with the skills and knowledge required to develop and implement innovative technologies and infrastructure projects. This is crucial for achieving sustainable development goals such as affordable and clean energy, sustainable cities and communities, and responsible consumption and production.

Moreover, Technical Education provides opportunities for students from diverse backgrounds to acquire skills and knowledge, enhancing their employability and income-earning potential. This, in turn, is crucial for reducing inequalities and promoting social inclusion. Additionally, Technical Education plays a critical role in advancing climate action by equipping students with the skills and knowledge required to develop and implement sustainable technologies and practices. This is crucial for achieving sustainable development goals such as climate action and clean water and sanitation.

Finally, Technical Education fosters partnerships between industry, academia, and government, promoting collaboration and knowledge-sharing. This is essential for achieving sustainable development goals that require concerted efforts from multiple stakeholders.

To maximize the impact of Technical Education on sustainable development goals, several strategies can be implemented.

- Technical Education curriculum should be updated to reflect the latest technological advancements and sustainable development goals. Technical educational institutions are instrumental in providing skills training and education that align with the needs of industries and the job market. They can contribute to reducing unemployment and under employment by producing a workforce with the necessary technical skills and competencies, fostering economic growth and contributing to SDG 8.

- Technical Education institutions should foster partnerships with industry, promoting knowledge-sharing and collaboration. Industry experts can provide practical learning experiences to students, enhancing their employability and promoting sustainable development. It contributes to SDG 9 (industry, innovation, and infrastructure) by developing and disseminating technologies that support sustainable technological and industrial development and SDG 12 (responsible consumption and production) by promoting and fostering eco-friendly and efficient technologies.

- Technical Education institutions should prioritize research and development activities that promote sustainable development. This can include the development of sustainable technologies and practices and the implementation of sustainable infrastructure projects. The themes identified under the Initiative on Critical and Emerging Technology (ICET) have also been adopted by AICTE. **The iCET themes are:**

1. Advanced Materials, Rare-earth & Critical Minerals
2. Semiconductors
4. Space and Defence
5. Blue Economy
6. Energy, Sustainability & Climate Change
7. Advanced Computing (Supercomputing, AI, Quantum Computing)
8. Next Gen Communications
9. Smart Cities & Mobility
10. Agritech & Food processing
11. Health Care & Medtech
12. Disaster Management & Resilient Infrastructure
13. Manufacturing & Industry 4.0

- Technical Education institutions should adopt sustainable campus practices, promoting energy and water conservation, waste reduction, and the use of renewable energy sources. They should be encouraged to become Net Zero campuses.

- Technical institutions should engage and partner with local communities to address specific challenges related to poverty (SDG 1), hunger (SDG 2), health and well-being (SDG 3), gender equality (SDG 5), and reduced inequalities (SDG 10).

- By involving and facilitating community development projects and initiatives, technical institutions contribute to the overall well-being of society, addressing multiple SDGs simultaneously.

7. ENHANCING ROLE OF GOVT. & TECHNICAL EDUCATION IN NATION BUILDING

Technical Education has emerged as a vital element in India's quest for sustainable development, owing to its massive population and burgeoning economy. Given the need for a robust Technical and Management Education system, the government has stepped up its efforts to build one. This vision document aims to delve into the role of the government in enhancing the role of Technical Education in nation-building. The government has been proactive in its efforts to build a strong Technical Education system.

- To this end, it has launched various initiatives, including the **National Skill Development Mission,** aimed at providing vocational education and training to over 400 million individuals by 2022. This initiative has been designed to address the skills gap and enhance employability among the Indian workforce based on the NSQF framework.
- Furthermore, the **Skill India Mission**, launched in 2015, aims to provide skills training to over 10 million young people by 2020, promoting entrepreneurship and job creation to fuel sustainable economic growth. The government has also initiated programs like the Atal Innovation Mission and the Start-up India initiative to promote innovation and entrepreneurship among students.
- To enhance the quality of Technical Education, the government has established the All India Council for Technical Education (AICTE), responsible for ensuring the quality of Technical Education in India. The AICTE has implemented several measures, such as the National Board of Accreditation, to accredit Technical Education institutions in India and National Institutional Ranking Framework for ranking quality institutions.
- The government has also rolled out policies aimed at promoting Technical Education in India. The National Education Policy 2020, approved in July 2020, is a landmark policy that seeks to transform the education system in India. The policy emphasizes the need to promote multidisciplinary education, vocational education, and experiential learning. It also stresses the importance of research and development activities in Technical Education institutions.

To build a robust Technical Education system, the government should adopt a multi-pronged strategy. It should increase funding for Technical Education institutions, ensuring that students have access to the latest technological advancements and learning resources.

The government should also facilitate collaborations between Technical Education institutions, industry, and government, promoting cross- fertilization of ideas and expertise. Industry experts can provide practical learning experiences to students, enhancing their employability and promoting sustainable development.

The government must also leverage emerging technologies like artificial intelligence, machine learning, and the internet of things in Technical Education. It should foster an ecosystem that promotes innovation and entrepreneurship, promoting job creation and sustainable economic growth. By implementing these strategies, the government can build a strong Technical Education system that supports sustainable development and boosts the role of Technical Education in nation-building.

8. BEST PRACTICES IN TECHNICAL EDUCATION FROM AROUND THE WORLD

Technical Education is a rapidly expanding field that is gaining momentum worldwide as nations seek to build a skilled workforce capable of contributing to their economic growth and development. Countries across the globe are embracing different approaches to Technical Education.

- **Finland,** a country renowned for its outstanding Technical Education system, has invested in a robust vocational education and training system that offers a pathway to higher education, including doctoral degrees. The Finnish system emphasizes practical, hands-on learning that prepares students for the workforce. With access to cutting-edge facilities, equipment, and technology, students are taught by highly qualified and experienced instructors. Additionally, the Finnish government has implemented policies that encourage collaboration between industry, government, and academia, promoting the exchange of knowledge and expertise.

- In **Singapore,** the Technical and Vocational Education and Training (TVET) system is widely recognized for its quality and efficacy. The Singaporean government has made substantial investments in modern infrastructure, equipment, and technology, providing students with practical learning experiences. The TVET system in Singapore is designed to cater to the needs of industry, ensuring that graduates are highly employable. To achieve this, the government collaborates closely with industry to develop and implement training programs tailored to specific industries.

- **Germany** is another country with an exceptionally effective Technical Education system. The German dual education system combines vocational training in companies with classroom education in vocational schools. This approach provides students with hands-on experience and theoretical knowledge. The German government works closely with industry to develop training programs that align with industry needs. Additionally, the government provides financial incentives to companies that participate in the dual education system, thereby encouraging them to train and employ young people.

- **China** is fast emerging as a global leader in Technical Education. The country has made significant investments in Technical Education infrastructure, providing state-of-the-art facilities, equipment, and technology. The Chinese government has implemented policies that promote collaboration between industry and academia, ensuring that training programs are designed to meet the needs of industry. Furthermore, the Chinese government encourages entrepreneurship and innovation, providing financial and other incentives to students who venture into business.

- The **United States of America** boasts a highly developed Technical Education system, with community colleges playing a significant role in providing vocational education and training. The community college system provides affordable education and training to students, preparing them for a wide range of technical careers. The U.S. government also provides financial aid to students who cannot afford to pay for their education, making Technical Education accessible to all.

Technical Education is an expanding field that is gaining momentum globally. Finland, Singapore, Germany, China, and the United States are some of the countries that have developed highly effective Technical Education systems. The best practices in Technical Education from around the world include hands-on learning, modern infrastructure, and collaboration between industry, government, and academia, alignment with industry needs, entrepreneurship, and innovation. By learning from and adapting these best practices, countries can build strong Technical Education systems that prepare students for the workforce, enhance their employability, and contribute to sustainable economic growth and development.

9. NEED FOR CURRICULUM REFORM & BUILDING ROBUST RESEARCH & INNOVATION ECOSYSTEM

The dire need for curriculum reform and the establishment of a robust research ecosystem to foster innovation and development cannot be overemphasized. These two critical elements are fundamental components for creating an environment that facilitates innovation and development.

Curriculum Reform is an absolute necessity if we want education to be in sync with the needs of the economy, industry and society. Outdated curricula that do not align with the demands of the workforce can lead to a skills mismatch, high unemployment rates, and low productivity. Furthermore, a curriculum lacking in holistic development can result in students lacking the soft skills required for success in the workforce.

- The National Education Policy 2020 recognizes the need for curriculum reform and proposes the development of the **National Higher Education Qualification Framework (NHEQF)** for Higher Education including Technical Education, **National Skills Qualification Framework (NSQF)** for Vocational Education, Training & Skilling and **National Curriculum Framework (NCF)** for School Education to provide a comprehensive roadmap for this reform with an aim to ensure that the curriculum is relevant, comprehensive, and aligned with the needs of the economy and society.

Building a **Robust Research and Innovation Ecosystem** is equally critical to fostering innovation and development. Research and development (R&D) are the backbone of innovation as they provide the knowledge and expertise necessary to develop new products, services, and technologies. R&D is also instrumental in developing human capital by providing researchers with opportunities to develop new skills and knowledge.

- The NEP2020 emphasizes the significance of building a robust research ecosystem and proposes several measures to achieve this goal. The policy suggests establishing the National Research Foundation **(ANRF)**, which will fund and promote research in various fields. In line with the same, "Anusandhan" National Research Foundation **(ANRF)** has been introduced which will define the stature of India at 2047. The **ANRF** will provide grants to students and researchers to conduct research in areas of national importance.
- Additionally, the policy proposes establishing research parks and incubation centers to provide a platform for researchers to develop and commercialize their innovations.
- To further strengthen research and development, NEP2020 proposes introducing interdisciplinary research programs that encourage collaboration between different fields. The policy also aims to promote international collaboration in research and development by establishing partnerships with international institutions.
- Ministry of Education's Innovation Cell (MIC) at AICTE focuses on creating complete ecosystem which foster the culture of Innovation across all educational institutions from ideas generation to pre-incubation, incubation and graduating from the incubator as successful start-ups. MIC has so far conducted many activities of innovation and start-ups in the form of hackathons.

Curriculum reform and building a robust research and Innovation ecosystem are indispensable when it comes to fostering innovation and development. The National Education Policy 2020 recognizes the importance of these elements and proposes several initiatives to achieve them. By implementing these initiatives, India can develop a workforce that is skilled, innovative, and ready to take on the challenges of the future.

10. ENHANCING QUALITY OF TECHNICAL EDUCATION THROUGH ACCREDITATION AND QUALITY ASSURANCE

Technical Education plays a crucial role in shaping the future of any nation. It equips students with the knowledge and skills necessary to excel in the workforce and contribute to the economy. However, the quality of Technical Education in India has often been criticized for being inadequate. One way to address this issue is by implementing accreditation and quality assurance measures.

Accreditation is the process of evaluating the quality of an educational institution or program. It involves a rigorous assessment of various parameters such as curriculum, faculty, infrastructure, student outcomes, and governance. Accreditation ensures that an educational institution or program meets the set standards of quality and excellence.

Quality assurance, on the other hand, involves ongoing monitoring and evaluation of the educational process to ensure that the desired outcomes are achieved. Quality assurance measures include student feedback, teacher evaluations, program reviews, and continuous improvement initiatives.

The **National Board of Accreditation (NBA)** and the **National Assessment and Accreditation Council (NAAC)** are the two main accreditation bodies in India. NBA accredits Technical Education programs, while NAAC accredits higher education institutions. Accreditation by these bodies is crucial as it provides recognition and credibility to educational institutions and programs. It also helps students make informed decisions about their educational choices.

NEP2020 recognizes the importance of accreditation and quality assurance in enhancing the quality of Technical Education. It proposes the following;

- Establishment of the Higher Education Commission of India (HECI), which will be responsible for accreditation, regulation, and act as a standard setting body of higher education institutions. The HECI will replace the University Grants Commission (UGC) and the All India Council for Technical Education (AICTE).
- Emphasizes the need for a shift from input-based to outcome-based accreditation. Input-based accreditation focuses on inputs such as infrastructure and faculty, while outcome-based accreditation focuses on the desired outcomes such as student learning and employability. The policy proposes the development of a National Higher Education Qualification Framework (NHEQF) to align the accreditation process with the desired outcomes.
- Proposes the establishment of a National Assessment Council (NAC) to conduct periodic assessments of higher education institutions. The NAC will assess various aspects such as student learning outcomes, teaching quality, and research output.
- Proposes the establishment of Faculty Development Centers (FDCs) to provide training and development opportunities to faculty members. The FDCs will focus on developing the pedagogical skills of faculty members, promoting research and innovation, and promoting interdisciplinary collaboration.

AICTE has undertaken measures for Technology enablement of centralized standardized data collection for accreditation and underlying software for making the processes transparent and efficient (One Nation One Data - ONOD).

Accreditation and quality assurance measures are crucial to enhancing the quality of Technical Education in India. The National Education Policy 2020 recognizes the importance of these measures and proposes several initiatives to implement them. By implementing these measures, India can develop a robust Technical Education system that produces skilled and competent graduates who can contribute to the growth and development of the nation.

11. ATTRACTING AND RETAINING TALENTED FACULTY FOR TECHNICAL EDUCATION

The quality of education in Technical Education institutions depends significantly on the caliber of faculty. Talented and experienced faculty members play a crucial role in shaping the academic excellence of students and institutions. However, attracting and retaining such faculty members is a daunting task for most institutions, especially given the stiff competition for talented individuals in the job market. This vision document explores the challenges faced by Technical Education institutions in attracting and retaining talented faculty and proposes strategies to address these challenges.

The National Education Policy 2020 highlights the importance of attracting and retaining talented faculty members in Technical Education institutions. The policy recognizes that faculty members play a vital role in the development of the curriculum, pedagogy, and research activities. Therefore, the policy emphasizes the need to,

- Attract and retain high-quality faculty members by providing them with attractive salaries, benefits, and career progression opportunities.

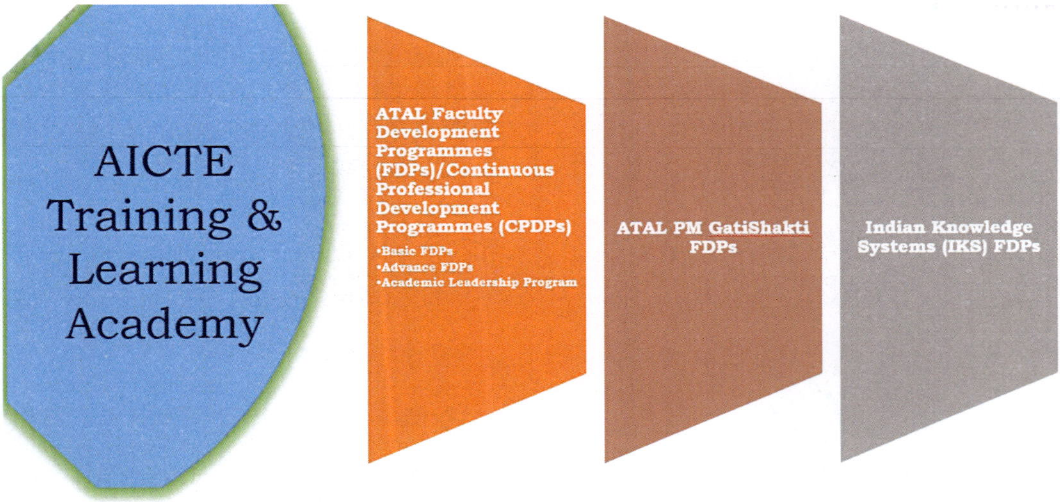

The role of teachers has evolved significantly over the time. The teachers are now the new facilitators for the students. The shift from being a traditional instructor to a facilitator reflects a more modern approach to education. Teachers as facilitators not just impart the knowledge and information but also guide and support students in their learning process by adapting teaching methods to suit diverse learning styles.

- Proposes the establishment of a National Mission for Mentoring, which will provide mentorship and guidance to new and young faculty members to help them achieve their full potential.

One of the significant challenges faced by Technical Education institutions in attracting and retaining faculty members is the **lack of adequate compensation** and benefits. Many institutions fail to offer competitive salaries, health insurance, retirement benefits, and other perks that are crucial in attracting and retaining talented individuals. Therefore, institutions must offer attractive compensation packages that align with industry standards to attract and retain talented faculty members.

Another challenge is the **lack of career progression opportunities.** Many faculty members do not see a clear path for career advancement in their current institutions, which leads to dissatisfaction and turnover. Therefore, institutions must provide career growth opportunities such as promotions, tenure, and opportunities for research and professional development.

The All India Council for Technical Education (AICTE) has also introduced several initiatives to attract and retain talented faculty members. For instance, the AICTE has established a **Faculty Development Programme (FDP)** to provide training and professional development opportunities for faculty members. The program aims to enhance the teaching, research, and leadership skills of faculty members and provide them with exposure to the latest developments in their respective fields. This concerted effort in teacher training shall therefore promote faculty certifications through 8 modules.

The mission is to promote the continuous efforts and encourage collaborations to provide funding for research projects, conferences and also for professional development certifications. This support enhances the faculty's expertise and keeps them engaged in scholarly activities aligning with global and local market requirements and trends.

Attracting and retaining talented faculty members is critical to the success of Technical Education institutions. Institutions must offer attractive compensation packages, career growth opportunities, and professional development programs to retain faculty members. The National Education Policy 2020 and the initiatives introduced by the AICTE provide a roadmap for institutions to attract and retain talented faculty members. By implementing these strategies, institutions can attract and retain talented individuals and create a thriving academic ecosystem.

FACULTY DEVELOPMENT PROGRAMME

12. DEVELOPING SKILLED & JOB-READY WORKFORCE THROUGH TECHNICAL EDUCATION

The dynamic world of work is constantly evolving, and it is imperative that our approach to education evolves with it. Technical Education plays a critical role in the development of a skilled and job-ready workforce that can adeptly respond to the demands of the 21st-century economy. It is crucial to align Technical Education with the requirements of the workforce and industry and to ensure that graduates possess the necessary skills to excel in their chosen fields.

The National Education Policy 2020 recognizes the vital role of Technical Education in developing a skilled workforce and proposes various initiatives to achieve this objective. The policy recommends the establishment of the **National Educational Technology Forum (NETF)** to facilitate the integration of technology into education. The NETF will also focus on creating a framework for the development of online and digital education, enabling learners to acquire new skills anytime and anywhere, thus reaching a broader audience.

The All India Council for Technical Education (AICTE) is a pivotal player in shaping Technical Education in India. The AICTE has recently implemented several measures to enhance the quality of Technical Education and improve student outcomes. One such measure is the **National Educational Alliance for Technology (NEAT)** program, which aims to provide students with industry-relevant skills through a range of online courses.

In addition, attracting and retaining talented faculty is also critical to the success of Technical Education institutions. The National Education Policy 2020 recognizes the need to create a more conducive environment for faculty members by providing them with professional development opportunities, research support, and better working conditions. The policy proposes the establishment of a **National Mission on Mentoring** to provide mentorship and support to faculty members.

Moreover, the National Education Policy 2020 recognizes the importance of providing students with practical experience through internships, apprenticeships, and on-the-job training. The policy recommends the establishment of a **National Apprenticeship Training System (NATS)** to provide students with opportunities to gain hands-on experience in various industries. The NATS will also focus on providing skill training to students in emerging sectors such as artificial intelligence, robotics, and data analytics. The dedicated platform for Apprenticeship, NATS Portal therefore enables students to gain professional experience while providing vital industry connect wherein business talent and skill requirements can be embedded within the Indian Technical Education domain.

The **AICTE Internship Portal** is a crucial aspect of developing a skilled and job-ready workforce through Technical Education. The portal aims to bridge the gap between industry and academia by providing students with hands-on experience and practical exposure to the industry. The AICTE Internship Portal is a user-friendly platform that connects students with leading companies and organizations for internships. The portal is an initiative under the National Education Policy 2020, which emphasizes the importance of practical training and internships in Technical Education.

- Through the AICTE Internship Portal, students can find internships in various fields such as engineering, management, pharmacy, architecture, and many more. The portal also provides students with opportunities to work on live projects, which can enhance their skills and knowledge.

- Furthermore, the AICTE Internship Portal provides companies with access to a pool of talented students who can contribute to their projects and initiatives. Companies can post their internship requirements on the portal, and students can apply for these internships based on their interests and skill sets.

- The AICTE Internship Portal also provides students with a unique opportunity to network with industry professionals and gain valuable insights into the corporate world. Students can interact with professionals from different industries and learn about the latest trends and developments in their field of interest.

The AICTE Internship Portal is an excellent initiative that can help in developing a skilled and job-ready workforce through Technical Education. The portal provides students with practical training and exposure to the industry, which can enhance their skills and knowledge. By connecting students with leading companies and organizations, the AICTE Internship Portal can help in bridging the gap between industry and academia.

Apart from Internship portal, the Vision is to focus on following areas to create a skilled and job read work force through technical higher education;

- Designing technical programs that are adaptable and responsive to the rapidly changing needs of industries across the globe

- Engage and foster partnerships with global institutions and industries to create opportunities for student exchanges, joint research projects, and collaborative initiatives.

- Training in cross-cultural communication, adversity quotient and global teamwork into the curriculum. This helps students develop the interpersonal skills, adaptability skills and critical thinking skills necessary for working in multicultural teams, a common aspect of the global workforce.

- Provide professional career counseling services and mentorship programs by making it mandatory in all technical higher educational institutions. Professional mentoring resources help students navigate their career paths, make informed decisions, and connect with industry professionals who can offer guidance based on their own experiences.

- Encourage collaborative research projects between academia and industry. These projects should address practical problems faced by industries, fostering a culture of applied innovation and make students and faculties work on relevant, cutting-edge technologies.

The **AICTE Placement Portal**, is a transformative platform to provide employment opportunities specially to village and tribal area students. The placement portal is a powerful tool to help bridge the gap between urban and rural areas in terms of access to employment opportunities. AICTE launched the 'AICTE Placement Portal' with the aim of aiding students in rural and tribal areas in their pursuit of equal job opportunities. This portal helps in eliminating the need for students in rural and tribal regions, especially those pursuing technical courses like engineering, to extensively search for jobs. It will directly connect them with numerous multinational companies, Industries, and other employers for job opportunities and providing them with the resources they need to succeed in the job market.

13. ADDRESSING ISSUES OF EQUITY, DIVERSITY AND INCLUSION IN TECHNICAL EDUCATION

The world of Technical Education is constantly evolving, and it is imperative to address issues of equity, diversity, and inclusion to ensure that every individual has access to quality education and employment opportunities. The National Education Policy 2020 and the All India Council for Technical Education (AICTE) recognize the importance of promoting equity, diversity, and inclusion in Technical Education and have proposed several initiatives to achieve this goal.

The NEP 2020 emphasizes the need for educational institutions to provide equal opportunities for all students, regardless of their socio-economic background, gender, or location. The policy proposes establishing a **Gender Inclusion Fund** to support initiatives that promote gender equity in education. The policy also emphasizes the need to provide adequate infrastructure, resources, and support to institutions located in rural areas to promote accessibility and inclusivity.

The AICTE has also introduced several measures to promote equity, diversity, and inclusion in Technical Education. The council has developed an e- learning platform called **SWAYAM**, which provides free online courses and study material to learners across the country. The AICTE has also established the **National Educational Alliance for Technology (NEAT)** program, which provides access to industry-relevant courses and skill training to students from diverse backgrounds.

In addition to these initiatives, the AICTE has also introduced a program called the **Margdarshan Scheme,** which provides guidance and mentorship to students from underprivileged backgrounds. The scheme aims to address the challenges faced by students from economically and socially marginalized backgrounds by providing them with the necessary guidance and support to pursue Technical Education.

Moreover, the AICTE has recognized the importance of promoting diversity and inclusion among faculty members. The council has introduced several measures to attract and retain faculty members from diverse backgrounds and to promote a culture of inclusivity and diversity within Technical Education institutions.

The AICTE has also recognized the importance of providing students with practical experience and exposure to diverse cultures and perspectives. The council has proposed establishing an **International Students' Cell** to promote internationalization and diversity within Technical Education institutions.

The NEP 2020 and the AICTE have also emphasized the importance of promoting entrepreneurship and innovation among students from diverse backgrounds. The policy proposes establishing an **Innovation and Entrepreneurship Development Centre (IEDC)** in every Technical Education institution to provide students with the necessary support and guidance to pursue entrepreneurial ventures.

Addressing issues of equity, diversity, and inclusion in Technical Education is essential to ensure that every individual has access to quality education and employment opportunities.

For that, initiatives such as

- Establish dedicated offices or centers to focus on diversity and inclusion. Aim is to organize events, workshops, and training sessions, as well as serve as resources for students and faculty seeking support or guidance.
- To establish partnerships with higher secondary and vocational higher secondary schools as well as community organizations to create pipeline programs that expose underrepresented as well as high potential students to STEM fields early on. This can include mentorship programs, workshops, and hands-on experiences to spark interest and confidence in pursuing technical education.
- Conduct regular cultural competence training for staff, faculty, and administrators to create a more inclusive and understanding campus culture. This training can promote awareness, reduce biases, and foster an environment where everyone feels valued and respected.

The NEP 2020 and the AICTE have recognized the importance of promoting equity, diversity, and inclusion in Technical Education and have proposed several initiatives to achieve this goal. By implementing these measures, India can develop a workforce that is diverse, inclusive, and equipped to meet the demands of the 21st-century economy.

14. LEVERAGING TECHNOLOGY TO ENHANCE TEACHING AND LEARNING IN TECHNICAL EDUCATION

The field of Technical Education has witnessed a remarkable transformation with the emergence of cutting-edge technologies. The integration of technology in education can significantly enhance the learning experience for students and improve the quality of education.

The National Education Policy 2020 recognizes the paramount significance of technology in education and proposes several initiatives to leverage technology to **enhance teaching and learning in Technical Education.** The policy emphasizes the need to create an inclusive educational environment that can reach a broad audience and promote equitable access to quality education. The policy underscores the establishment of the National Educational Technology Forum (NETF) to promote the integration of technology in education. The NETF will also foster the development of online and digital education, which can provide learners with anytime, anywhere learning opportunities.

The All India Council for Technical Education (AICTE) has launched a **Digital Skilling initiative to upskill 1 crore students and faculty.** The initiative aims to equip students and faculty with the necessary digital skills to adapt to the rapidly changing demands of the 21st-century economy. The initiative encompasses a range of online courses in programming, data analytics, artificial intelligence, and machine learning. These courses are meticulously designed to provide students with industry-relevant skills, thereby improving their employability and competitiveness in the job market.

The **Anuvadini** Artificial Intelligence text, video, and voice translation tool is an innovative technology that has the potential to revolutionize the way Technical Education is delivered. This state-of-the-art tool employs advanced machine learning algorithms to provide real-time translation of text, video, and voice content.

- The tool supports over 100 languages, making it an ideal solution for delivering education in multilingual environments.
- The Anuvadini AI tool can provide a seamless learning experience for students who are not fluent in the language of instruction. The tool can translate lectures, course materials, and other educational content in real-time, enabling students to understand and engage with the material more effectively.
- The tool can also provide translation services for faculty members, enabling them to communicate with students who speak different languages.
- The Anuvadini AI tool can also be used to create multilingual educational content. Faculty members can use the tool to create content in different languages, thereby promoting the accessibility and inclusivity of education.
- The tool can also translate existing educational content into different languages, enabling institutions to reach a broader audience.

By leveraging technology to enhance teaching and learning in Technical Education, we can improve the quality of education and make it more **accessible and inclusive.** The National Education Policy 2020 and the AICTE have recognized the critical role of technology in education and proposed several initiatives to leverage technology to enhance teaching and learning in Technical Education. The Anuvadini Artificial Intelligence text, video, and voice translation tool and the digital skilling initiative are exemplary initiatives that demonstrate the potential of technology to transform education. By embracing these initiatives, India can develop a workforce that is not only skilled but also adaptable and capable of driving innovation and growth in the economy.

15. IMPORTANCE OF INDUSTRY-ACADEMIA COLLABORATION IN TECHNICAL EDUCATION

In the dynamic and ever-evolving realm of Technical Education, the symbiotic relationship between industry and academia holds paramount significance. The exigencies of the current labour market necessitate a workforce that is competent, skilled and adaptable to the rapidly changing technological landscape. In this context, industry-academia collaboration in Technical Education becomes an imperative that cannot be overemphasized. By sharing knowledge, expertise and resources, industry and academia can synergize and create a formidable partnership that can drive innovation, growth and success.

The benefits of industry-academia collaboration are manifold. For academic institutions, it provides exposure to the latest developments in the industry and enables them to update their curriculum, ensuring that their graduates are equipped with industry-relevant skills. Industry experts can also share their practical knowledge and expertise with students, helping them develop a practical understanding of the real-world applications of Technical Education.

For the industry, collaboration with academic institutions provides **access to the latest research**

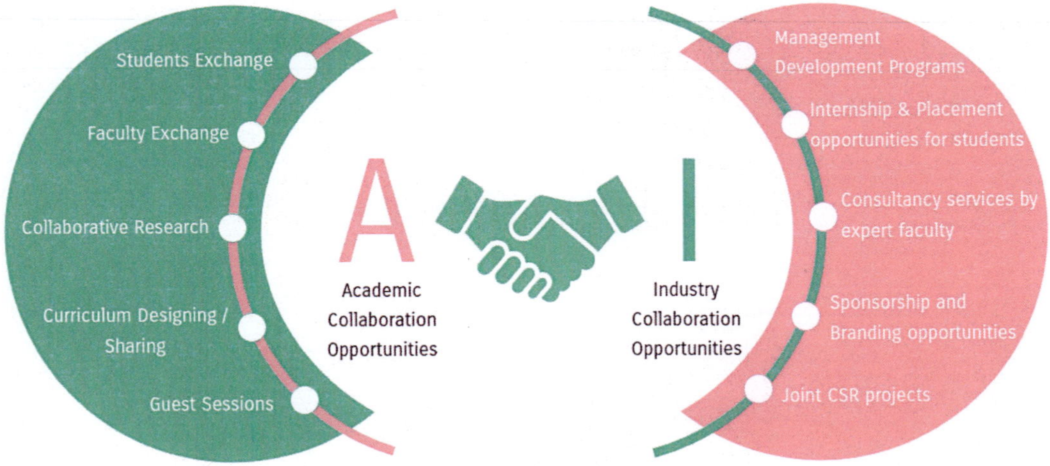

and development, enabling them to stay at the forefront of their respective domains. It also allows them to **tap into the potential of the next generation of talent,** who can bring fresh perspectives, ideas, and innovation to the table. The industry can also leverage the research output of academic institutions to develop new products, technologies and services. The benefits of industry-academia collaboration can be further enhanced by leveraging technology. In this context, digital skilling initiatives, such as the

The symbiotic relationship between industry and academia has been well- established, and it is a quintessential component of the modern economy. In Technical Education, this relationship assumes particular significance, as it **allows academic institutions to align their curriculum and research with the demands of the industry.** The industry, on the other hand, can **leverage the expertise and research output of academic institutions to drive innovation, develop new products, and solve complex challenges.**

ones proposed by AICTE, can play a pivotal role in fostering collaboration between industry and academia. These initiatives can enable academic institutions to provide industry-relevant skills comprising of equal contribution of practical and theory (50% each) to their students making them more employable and adaptive to the needs of the industry. They can also provide the industry with access to a vast pool of skilled talent, which can fuel innovation and growth.

Further, AICTE mandatory Training and Placement Cells and AICTE Internship and Placement Portal help empower institutions, students and teachers to collaborate with local industry in order to generate long term employment opportunities.

The importance of industry-academia collaboration in Technical Education cannot be overstated.

Our vision document highlights the significance of :

- Structured internship programs and cooperative education initiatives that enable students to gain real-world experience in industry settings. Collaborate with local businesses and industries to identify opportunities for students to apply their theoretical knowledge in practical settings as well help them learn the new skills and competences required for a practical work environment.
- Encourage industry professionals to participate in designing and supervising the internship and project programs, providing students with mentorship and insights into current industry practices.
- Encourage faculty members to engage in professional development activities, such as product development projects or quick applied research projects as per the needs of the industry or short-term assignments in industry, to stay updated on the latest advancements and challenges in the field.
- Create an induction loop between the industry and academia, allowing prospective employers to provide inputs on the skills and competencies they require in prospective workforce, helping to tailor the curriculum to meet industry needs.
- By collaborating and sharing knowledge, expertise, and resources, industry and academia can create a formidable partnership that can drive innovation, growth and success.

The symbiotic relationship between industry and academia has the potential to create a win-win situation for all stakeholders, and it is imperative that we leverage this relationship to the fullest. By doing so, we can create a workforce that is not only skilled but also adaptable and capable of driving innovation and growth in the economy.

16. PROMOTING ENTREPRENEURSHIP AND START-UP CULTURE THROUGH TECHNICAL EDUCATION

In this era of economic development, entrepreneurship has become a driving force for growth and innovation. In order to promote entrepreneurship and create a start-up culture, it is crucial to provide a conducive environment for the development of entrepreneurial skills. Technical Education can play a significant role in nurturing these skills among students and facilitating their transition from being job seekers to job creators. The National Education Policy 2020 recognizes the importance of entrepreneurship and proposes several initiatives to promote it. Entrepreneurship is not just about starting a business but also about **creating solutions to problems and identifying new opportunities.** Technical Education can help students develop the skills necessary to become successful entrepreneurs. It provides students with the necessary knowledge and skills to identify problems and develop innovative solutions to address them. Technical Education can also help students learn how to **manage a business, develop a business plan, and secure funding.**

The National Education Policy 2020 recognizes the importance of entrepreneurship and proposes several initiatives to promote it. The policy aims to create an environment that is conducive to the development of entrepreneurship skills among students. It proposes the **establishment of incubation centers in higher education institutions** to support start-ups and promote entrepreneurship. The policy also encourages the **development of start-up hubs and innovation centers** in the country to provide support and mentoring to aspiring entrepreneurs.

In addition to the National Education Policy 2020, several other initiatives have been launched to promote entrepreneurship and start-up culture in India. The **Start-up India program** is one such initiative that provides funding and mentoring support to start-ups. The program aims to create a network of start-ups and incubators to support and nurture the growth of new businesses. The **Atal Innovation Mission** and **Ministry of Education's Innovation Cell (MIC)** is another initiative that aims to promote innovation and entrepreneurship among students.

Technical Education can play a vital role in promoting entrepreneurship and start-up culture. It can equip students with the necessary skills and knowledge to create innovative solutions to problems and identify new opportunities. The National Education Policy 2020 and other initiatives provide a conducive environment for the development of entrepreneurial skills among students. By nurturing these skills, India can create a generation of job creators who can drive innovation and economic growth in the country.

Going forward, technical higher educational institutions must focus on following points to foster best in class start up ecosystem culture: -

- Programs on comprehensive entrepreneurship curriculum that includes courses on business planning, human resources management, organizational behavior, financial management, supply chain management, marketing, and innovation connecting multiple technical domains
- Encourage collaboration between different technological streams and global exchange programs to promote interdisciplinary projects and startup ideas.
- Further enhance the system for seed funding and grants to support student-led startup initiatives

- Provide resources and guidance on legal and regulatory aspects of starting and running a business. This includes information on intellectual property rights, business registration, and compliance.

AICTE focus on promoting entrepreneurial skills in technical education and believes it as the key component of long-term sustainable development. It helps build a foundation for economic stability, reduces unemployment, and promotes a culture of continuous learning and improvement.

PM Shri Narendra Modi visited ATAL stall at the inauguration of Akhil Bhartiya Shiksha Samagam at Bharat Mandapam, in New Delhi on July 29, 2023.

17. BUILDING A GLOBAL REPUTATION FOR TECHNICAL EDUCATION IN INDIA

Building a global reputation for Technical Education in India requires a sustained effort by all stakeholders, including the government, educational institutions, industry, and the community. It requires a commitment to excellence, a culture of innovation and entrepreneurship, and a willingness to embrace new technologies and approaches to education. The National Education Policy 2020 has laid the foundation for a new era of educational reform and technological innovation. The policy envisages a transformation in the way Technical Education is imparted in India, and it seeks to equip students with the knowledge, skills, and attitudes required to succeed in a rapidly evolving global economy.

The AICTE has been at the forefront of this transformative process, and it has taken several initiatives to enhance the quality of Technical Education in India and make it globally competitive. The AICTE has recognized that the future of Technical Education lies in its ability to foster a culture of innovation, creativity, and entrepreneurship. Therefore, the AICTE has launched several programs that aim to promote research and development, and innovation in Technical Education.

One of the key objectives of the National Education Policy 2020 is to build a global reputation for Technical Education in India. The policy recognizes that India has the potential to become a global leader in Technical Education, but it also acknowledges that there are several challenges that need to be addressed to realize this potential. These challenges include improving the quality of education, enhancing the employability of students, and fostering a culture of innovation and entrepreneurship.

To address these challenges, the National Education Policy 2020 proposes several measures, including the establishment of the National Educational Technology Forum (NETF), which will serve as a platform for promoting innovation in education and integrating technology into education. The NETF will also focus on developing online and digital education and creating a framework for the development of e-learning content.

Another important initiative proposed by the National Education Policy 2020 is the **establishment of Centres of Excellence in areas such as artificial intelligence, machine learning, and robotics.** These centres will provide students with opportunities to engage in research and development, and innovation in cutting-edge technologies. These centres will also collaborate with industry and other stakeholders to ensure that the research conducted in these areas is relevant to the needs of the industry and the economy.

The AICTE has also taken several steps to promote innovation and entrepreneurship in Technical Education. The AICTE has launched several programs, such as the Smart India Hackathon, which provides students with opportunities to engage in innovation and entrepreneurship. The AICTE has also established incubation centres to provide support to start-ups and entrepreneurial ventures.

AICTE also focus on global alumni network of Indian students, global rankings, industry partnerships, language and cultural exchange programs along with international research and innovation projects to enhance the image of technical education stream of our Country. AICTE International Cell will create a global reputation for excellence in Technical and Management Education.

By working together, we can transform Technical Education in India and build a global reputation for excellence and innovation.

18. ROLE OF NGOS, PRIVATE SECTOR IN TECHNICAL EDUCATION IN INDIA

The Technical Education system in India is currently undergoing a significant transformation. While the government and the All India Council for Technical Education (AICTE) have been the driving force behind the development of Technical Education, non-governmental organizations (NGOs) and private sector entities have played a crucial role in enhancing the quality and accessibility of Technical Education in India. This vision document will delve into the role played by NGOs and the private sector in Technical Education in India, with a particular focus on their contributions to the implementation of the National Education Policy 2020 and the AICTE's initiatives.

The National Education Policy 2020 and the AICTE's initiatives emphasize the need to enhance the quality and accessibility of Technical Education in India. The initiatives aim to equip students with industry-relevant skills and improve their employability. The policy recognizes the role of NGOs and the private sector in the development of Technical Education and proposes several measures to facilitate their involvement in the sector.

NGOs in Technical Education

NGOs have played a significant role in improving the quality and accessibility of Technical Education in India. They have been instrumental in implementing various programs and initiatives aimed at enhancing the skills and employability of students. NGOs have collaborated with educational institutions to offer skill-based training programs, vocational courses, and job-oriented programs. Many NGOs have also been actively involved in promoting innovation and entrepreneurship among students, providing them with mentorship, guidance, and financial support to launch their own start- ups.

The role of NGOs has become even more critical in light of the COVID-19 pandemic. Many NGOs have been at the forefront of providing online education and training programs to students who have been unable to attend physical classes due to the pandemic. They have also been involved in the distribution of digital devices to students who do not have access to such devices.

Private Sector in Technical Education

The private sector has also played a significant role in the development of Technical Education in India. Private educational institutions have emerged as major players in the sector, offering high-quality education and training programs to students. Many private institutions have collaborated with industry players to design courses and training programs that are tailored to the needs of the industry. The private sector has also been actively involved in promoting research and innovation in Technical Education, providing financial support and mentorship to students and faculty members.

The role of the private sector in Technical Education has become even more critical in light of the AICTE's initiatives to promote digital skilling and entrepreneurship. Private institutions have been at the forefront of developing and delivering online courses and training programs to students. They have also been actively involved in promoting entrepreneurship among students, providing them with mentorship, guidance, and financial support to launch their own start-ups.

Collaboration between NGOs, Private Sector and Government

Collaboration between NGOs, the private sector and the government is crucial to the development of Technical Education in India. The National Education Policy 2020 recognizes the importance of such collaboration and proposes several measures to facilitate it. The policy proposed the establishment of a 'Anusandhan' **National Research Foundation (ANRF)** to promote research and innovation in the education sector. The NRF will provide financial support to educational institutions and researchers, enabling them to undertake research and development projects that are relevant to the needs of the industry.

The policy also proposes the establishment of an **Academic Bank of Credit (ABC)** to facilitate the transfer of credits between educational institutions. The ABC will enable students to pursue interdisciplinary courses and programs, providing them with a broader range of skills and knowledge. The ABC will also facilitate the transfer of credits earned by students in foreign institutions, enabling them to pursue further studies or work opportunities abroad.

NGOs and the private sector have played a significant role in enhancing the quality and accessibility of Technical Education in India. Their contributions have been instrumental and shall be leveraged and engagement deepened in the coming years.

Going forward, technical educational institutions can partner with or empanel NGOs and private organizations in promoting the vision of technical higher education. The association could be multi-faceted, comprising financial support, infrastructure development, industry collaboration, skill development, advocacy, emotional and social well-being of students & teachers, global partnership, quality assurance and accreditation, entrepreneurial support, social and sustainable solutions and inventions etc. Their contributions can significantly enhance the overall quality and relevance of technical education, preparing students for successful careers in a rapidly evolving global landscape.

19. LEVERAGING DIGITAL PLATFORMS TO ENHANCE TECHNICAL EDUCATION

The world has become increasingly digital, and education is no exception. The advent of technology and its increasing ubiquity have paved the way for an unprecedented transformation in the education sector. India has been no exception, and the country has seen a significant rise in the use of digital platforms to enhance Technical Education. In this vision document, we will explore the impact of digital platforms on Technical Education and how the National Education Policy 2020, the All India Council for Technical Education (AICTE), the National Education Technology Forum (NETF), the APAAR (Automated Permanent Academic Account Registry), Digilocker, Academic Bank of Credits (ABC), and the National Digital Education Architecture (NDEAR) ecosystem are enabling this transformation.

The National Education Policy 2020 has emphasized the importance of digital education and aims to leverage technology to provide equitable and inclusive quality education to all. The policy envisions a comprehensive digital infrastructure that will provide universal access to quality education. The policy also aims to promote online learning and provide support for teacher training in digital pedagogy.

AICTE, the statutory body responsible for planning, formulation, and maintenance of norms and standards in Technical Education, has been at the forefront of leveraging digital platforms to enhance Technical Education. AICTE has launched several initiatives to enable digital learning, including the National Education Technology Forum (NETF). NETF is a platform for sharing best practices and resources related to technology in education. It also provides a collaborative platform for stakeholders to work together to develop new digital solutions for education.

The **APAAR (Automated Permanent Academic Account Registry)** is another initiative by Ministry of Education, which provides a unique identification number to students, faculty, and institutes using Digilocker, Academic Bank of Credits (ABC) and OpenAPIs. This registry will enable seamless integration of educational records across different systems and platforms, making it easier for students to access their academic records and for institutes to manage their data.

The **National Digital Education Architecture (NDEAR) ecosystem** is another initiative by the Ministry of Education, which aims to provide a comprehensive digital infrastructure for education. The ecosystem comprises several components, including the National Teacher Platform, the National Repository of Open Educational Resources, e-KUMBH, SWAYAM, the e-Content Creation and Dissemination Portal, and the **One Nation One Digital Platform.**

Leveraging the InDEA 2.0 framework, these initiatives have the potential to transform the Indian education system by providing universal access to quality education and enabling a seamless and integrated digital infrastructure. The APAAR (Automated Permanent Academic Account Registry), Digilocker, ABC, and NDEAR ecosystem are game-changers in the Indian education ecosystem and have the potential to transform the way we learn and teach.

The digital transformation of Technical Education in India is well underway, and the government, regulatory bodies, and private sector are working together to ensure that the country stays at the forefront of this revolution. Digilocker is a cloud-based platform that provides secure online storage of documents and certificates. It is an initiative of the Ministry of Electronics and Information Technology,

Government of India, and is available to all Indian citizens. Digilocker is an essential component of the APAAR (Automated Permanent Academic Account Registry), and it enables students to store and access their educational certificates and documents online.

Academic Bank of Credits (ABC) is another initiative, which enables students to earn credits for courses completed in any institute and accumulate them in a digital account. These credits can be transferred to another institute, and the students can continue their education without any loss of credits. ABC also provides a platform for institutes to share their course catalogues and make them accessible to students across the country.

e-KUMBH

Knowledge Unleased in Multiple Bharatiya Languages

Visit: https://ekumbh.aicte-india.org/index.php

20. DEVELOPING SUSTAINABLE INFRASTRUCTURE FOR TECHNICAL EDUCATION IN INDIA

Technical Education plays a vital role in the development of any nation. It not only equips students with the necessary skills and knowledge but also creates a workforce that can contribute to the growth of the economy. In India, the National Education Policy 2020 aims to reform the education system by promoting Technical Education and developing sustainable infrastructure. This vision document will discuss the importance of sustainable infrastructure in Technical Education and the strategies and implementation plans required to achieve it.

Sustainable infrastructure is the foundation of Technical Education. It includes physical facilities such as buildings, equipment, and laboratories, as well as digital infrastructure such as high-speed internet and software. Sustainable infrastructure is crucial for providing a conducive learning environment and promoting innovation and research.

However, developing sustainable infrastructure requires significant investment and planning. The government and educational institutions must work together to identify the key areas that require investment and prioritize them. The investment must be strategic and should aim to create long-term value. The development of sustainable infrastructure can also be an opportunity to promote sustainable practices and reduce the carbon footprint of educational institutions.

The development of sustainable infrastructure requires a comprehensive strategy that addresses the needs of educational institutions and their students. The following are some strategies that can be adopted to develop sustainable infrastructure in Technical Education:

- **Collaboration:** Collaboration between educational institutions and the government can help identify the key areas that require investment. It can also lead to the development of joint initiatives that promote sustainable infrastructure.
- **Public-Private Partnership:** Private sector involvement can provide additional funding and expertise to develop sustainable infrastructure. Public-private partnerships can also lead to the development of innovative solutions that are not possible through public funding alone.
- **Innovation:** Innovation can help reduce the cost of sustainable infrastructure development. New technologies and innovative solutions can help reduce the carbon footprint of educational institutions while improving the quality of education.
- **Sustainability:** The development of sustainable infrastructure should be aligned with sustainable development goals. Educational institutions should adopt sustainable practices in their operations and promote awareness among their students.

The **implementation plan for developing sustainable infrastructure** should be well-defined and executed efficiently. The following are some of the key steps that can be taken to implement the plan:

- **Assess the Current Infrastructure:** Educational institutions should assess their current infrastructure and identify the areas that require improvement. The assessment should include the physical and digital infrastructure.

- **Prioritize Investments:** The assessment should be used to prioritize investments. The investments should be aligned with the overall strategy for sustainable infrastructure development.
- **Identify Funding Sources:** The funding sources for the investments should be identified. This can include government funding, private funding, or public-private partnerships.
- **Develop a Roadmap:** A roadmap should be developed that outlines the timeline for the implementation of the investments. The roadmap should be realistic and achievable.

Developing sustainable infrastructure is crucial for the growth of Technical Education in India. It requires collaboration between the government, educational institutions, and the private sector. The strategies for developing sustainable infrastructure should focus on innovation, collaboration, and sustainability. The implementation plan should be well-defined and executed efficiently. By investing in sustainable infrastructure, India can develop a skilled workforce that can contribute to the growth of the economy while promoting sustainable practices.

AICTE mandated Institutional Development Scheme initiative focuses on ensuring upkeep of holistic institutional performance comprising of various institute level initiatives such as-

- Research Promotion Scheme to help drive institution level innovation.
- Entrepreneur Development Cell to promote student businesses.
- e-Shodhsindhu providing off campus remote access to online learning materials.
- Faculty Development Programme and internships to create pathways of career growth and individual improvement for teachers in Technical education.
- Margdarshan Scheme which has been recently launched in order to promote excellence in Technical Education whereby identified institutions shall mentor rural institutions that have not yet received accreditation. This shall provide the required handholding support and pathways for accreditation thereby benefiting the students in these regions.
- Unnat Bharat Abhiyan
- Mentor – Mentee Scheme
- Hostels for SC/ST Students
- Skill and Personality Development Centre for SC/ST Students.
- Multiple Fellowships and Scholarships for underserved students: Pragati, Saksham, PMSSS, ADF, QIP, M Tech Scholarship etc.

21. STRENGTHENING TECHNICAL EDUCATION IN EMERGING FIELDS SUCH AS AI, IOT, ROBOTICS, CYBER SECURITY, QUANTUM COMPUTING, DATA ANALYTICS, UI/UX

In today's era of rapid technological advancements, the world is witnessing a paradigm shift in the nature of work and the skills required to succeed. With the emergence of new and innovative fields such as Artificial Intelligence (AI), Internet of Things (IoT), Quantum computing, Cybersecurity, Data analytics, Robotics, and many more, the demand for technical expertise in these areas is rapidly increasing. The challenge, however, lies in ensuring that the **workforce of tomorrow is adequately trained to meet the demands of these emerging fields. This is where the role of Technical Education comes into play.**

The All India Council for Technical Education (AICTE) has been tasked with the responsibility of implementing these changes.

The AICTE, in collaboration with the National Education Technology Forum (NETF), has developed a comprehensive strategy to strengthen Technical Education in emerging fields. This strategy involves the **development of new courses and programs that are tailored to the needs of these emerging fields.** The implementation of this strategy will require a significant investment in infrastructure, faculty, and technology.

The National Education Policy 2020 recognizes the need to strengthen Technical Education in emerging fields such as AI, IoT, Cybersecurity, Robotics, etc. It aims to achieve this by developing a **multidisciplinary approach to education** that encourages the integration of various fields of study.

The implementation plan involves setting up specialized **centers of excellence in emerging fields that will serve as hubs for research, training, and development.** These centers of excellence will be equipped with state-of-the-art facilities and will have a dedicated team of faculty and researchers.

The aim is to create an ecosystem that promotes innovation, collaboration, and learning.

In addition to this, the AICTE and NETF are also working towards developing a **National Digital Education Architecture (NDEAR)** ecosystem that will provide a digital platform for students, faculty, and institutes. This platform will allow students to access their academic records, certificates, and other important documents through a unique ID provided by the APAAR (Automated Permanent Academic Account Registry). The NDEAR eco-system will also provide access to the Academic Bank of Credits (ABC) that will allow students to accumulate credits for courses completed and transfer them across institutions.

To further leverage the power of technology in enhancing Technical Education, the AICTE and NETF are working towards the application of the India 2.0 framework. This framework aims to provide a comprehensive approach to the development of Technical Education in India by leveraging technology to enhance the quality and relevance of education. The India 2.0 framework will also promote the development of soft skills such as communication, collaboration, and critical thinking, which are essential for success in today's world.

In conclusion, the need to strengthen Technical Education in emerging fields such as AI, IoT, Cybersecurity, Robotics, etc., cannot be overstated. The National Education Policy 2020 recognizes this need and has provided a roadmap for achieving this goal. The AICTE and NETF are working towards implementing this roadmap by developing a comprehensive strategy that involves the development of new courses and programs, specialized centers of excellence, and a digital platform for students, faculty, and institutes. The success of this strategy will require a significant investment in infrastructure, faculty, and technology. However, the rewards will be immense in terms of creating a workforce that is equipped with the skills needed to succeed in the emerging fields of tomorrow.

Skill India Digital is one such initiative of Ministry of Skill Development and Entrepreneurship which encompasses all skill related activities. Skill India Digital is specially designed and developed to skill, reskill and upskill Indian individuals through an online training platform. It acts as a bridge between the employees and employers and allow educational institutes to create/modify curricula as per industry demands. AICTE has also integrated with Skill India Digital for its Internship and Placement Portal.

22. BRIDGING THE SKILL GAP THROUGH APPRENTICESHIP AND INTERNSHIP PROGRAMS

In the current age of technology and innovation, there is a growing demand for highly skilled professionals in technical fields. However, there is a **persistent gap between the skills possessed by graduates and the skills required by the industry.** To address this issue, apprenticeship and internship programs have emerged as a promising solution. In this vision document, we will explore the importance of apprenticeship and internship programs in bridging the skill gap in Technical Education, as well as the role of the National Education Policy 2020 and the All India Council for Technical Education (AICTE) in promoting these programs.

Apprenticeship Programs

Apprenticeship programs provide students with an opportunity to **gain practical, on-the-job training in their field of study.** These programs allow students to apply theoretical knowledge to real-world scenarios and develop the skills required by the industry. Apprenticeship programs also provide students with an opportunity to network with industry professionals, gain exposure to different areas of their field, and receive guidance and mentorship from experienced professionals.

The National Education Policy 2020 recognizes the importance of apprenticeship programs and aims to promote them as a means of bridging the skill gap in Technical Education. The policy proposes the creation of a **National Apprenticeship Promotion Scheme (NAPS)** to provide financial incentives to employers to engage apprentices. The AICTE has also taken steps to promote apprenticeship programs by creating a **National Apprenticeship Training Scheme (NATS) portal,** which facilitates the recruitment of apprentices and the monitoring of their training.

Internship Programs

Internship programs provide students with an opportunity to gain practical experience in their field of study by working with organizations for a period of time. These programs allow students to apply theoretical knowledge to real-world scenarios, develop the skills required by the industry, and gain exposure to different areas of their field. Internship programs also provide students with an opportunity to network with industry professionals and gain insights into the industry. In order to achieve SDG goals, the social entrepreneurship needs to be encouraged.

The National Education Policy 2020 recognizes the importance of Industry professionals programs and aims to promote them as a means of bridging the skill gap in Technical Education. The policy proposes the creation of an **APAAR (Automated Permanent Academic Account Registry)**, which will provide a unique ID to students, faculty, and institutes. This registry will be linked to the Academic Bank of Credits (ABC) and will facilitate the recognition of credits earned by students through internships.

Implementation Plan

To implement apprenticeship and internship programs effectively, a comprehensive strategy is required. This strategy shall include the following steps:

- Identify the skill gaps in the industry and design apprenticeship and internship programs that address these gaps.
- Partner with industry organizations to

provide students with practical training opportunities.

- Provide students with guidance and mentorship to ensure that they develop the skills required by the industry.
- Establish mechanisms to monitor the progress of apprentices and interns and ensure that they are receiving high-quality training.
- Provide financial incentives to employers to engage apprentices and interns.

Apprenticeship and Internship programs have emerged as a promising solution to bridge the skill gap in Technical Education. The National Education Policy 2020 and the AICTE have recognized the importance of these programs and have taken steps to promote them. To implement these programs effectively, a comprehensive strategy is required that involves the identification of skill gaps, partnerships with industry organizations, guidance and mentorship for students, monitoring of progress, and financial incentives for employers. By promoting apprenticeship and internship programs, we can develop a skilled workforce that meets the demands of the industry and contributes to the growth of the economy.

The holistic focus to bridge the skill gap through internships and apprenticeship programs highlights the following areas:

- Continuous skills assessments to identify strengths as well as areas where students may need additional support. It may be used to tailor internship and apprenticeship programs to address specific skill gaps.
- Offer simulation labs, hackathons, and other experiential learning opportunities within the academic setting.
- Create virtual or augmented reality experiences that simulate real-world scenarios under the guidance core domain experts.
- Establish a continuous feedback loop between educational institutions and industry partners to ensure that the curriculum remains relevant.
- Organize networking events, career fairs, and industry seminars to facilitate interactions between students and potential employers.
- Encourage students to build professional connections during their internships.

23. ROLE OF INCUBATION CENTERS & ACCELERATORS IN SUPPORTING START-UPS

Technical Education is an important aspect of education that is necessary for economic development and growth. India, being a developing nation, has recognized the significance of Technical Education and has taken various steps to promote it. With the introduction of the National Education Policy (NEP) 2020, Technical Education has been given a new direction. One of the important aspects of NEP 2020 is to promote entrepreneurship and start-ups through Technical Education. This has given rise to the need for incubation centers and accelerators to support the start-up ecosystem in India.

The Innovation Council:

To promote innovation and entrepreneurship, NEP 2020 has established the Innovation Council. The council aims to identify and support innovative ideas that can lead to the creation of new products, services, and businesses. The Innovation Council works in collaboration with various stakeholders such as the government, industry, academia, and start-ups to promote innovation and entrepreneurship.

Why Startups Need Incubators/Accelerators?

1. Networking Opportunities
2. Access to Resources
3. Exposure to Industry Experts & Mentors
4. Access to Funding
5. Accelerate the Growth
6. Provides ecosystem to support

Role of Incubation Centers:

Incubation centers play a vital role in providing the necessary resources and support to start-ups. They provide a platform for the start-ups to grow and develop their ideas. Incubation centers are equipped with state-of-the-art facilities and infrastructure that help start-ups in their early stages. They provide access to mentors, industry experts, and funding agencies that help start-ups in their journey.

Role of Accelerators:

Accelerators provide a platform for start-ups to grow and scale their businesses. They provide access to funding, mentorship, and resources that help start-ups in their growth trajectory. Accelerators work with start-ups to refine their business models, develop their products, and market their offerings. They provide a network of contacts and connections that help start-ups in their journey.

Strategy and Implementation Plan:

The role of incubation centers and accelerators is critical in supporting start-ups through Technical Education. A strategy and implementation plan must be put in place to ensure the effective functioning of these centers. The strategy should focus on identifying the right start-ups and providing them with the necessary resources and support. The plan should focus on providing funding, mentorship, and resources that help start-ups in their journey.

The future of incubation centers and accelerators could focus on;

- Cultivating entrepreneurial mind set among students and teachers beyond traditional academic boundaries
- Cross Disciplinary collaboration from various disciplines
- Promoting Entrepreneur – in residence programs and industry mentors' involvement in startup project guidance
- Earning credits for vetted student startups in domain areas
- Community outreach projects to address local and global challenges and needs
- Continuous improvement with regular feedback mechanisms and agile approach

The role of incubation centers and accelerators is critical in supporting start- ups through Technical Education. NEP 2020 has recognized the importance of promoting entrepreneurship and start-ups through Technical Education. The Innovation Council and other stakeholders must work together to provide the necessary resources and support to start-ups. A strategy and implementation plan must be put in place to ensure the effective functioning of these centers. With the right support, start-ups can grow and develop into successful businesses, contributing to the economic growth and development of India, making it very critical for Viksit Bharat @ 2047.

AICTE promotes Innovation, a new-age learning :

AICTE INDOVATION CENTRES: Moving a step further from innovation to what has been termed as "indovation", the All India Council for Technical Education (AICTE) plans to set up eleven such centres across the country to carry out Indian Knowledge System (IKS) projects – a mainstay of the Centre's new education policy. The indovation centres will be set up in 11 cities including – Kanpur, Bhopal, Bengaluru, Trivandrum, Hyderabad, Chennai, Chandigarh, Jaipur, Baroda, Kolkata and Guwahati. These cells will be carrying out research for IKS projects such as validating theories developed in the ancient times, verifying old texts, carrying out translations, among others.

- **IIC Regional Meet:** It is a flagship programme of Ministry of Education's Innovation Cell (MIC), designed to provide a networking platform for IIC institutions and prospective IIC institutions to celebrate their contribution towards institutionalising and streamlining their campus innovation ecosystems and leading the innovation movement in Higher Education Institutions.
- **AICTE IDEA LABS:** AICTE introduced the concept of Idea lab to transform technical education by empowering young minds with cutting-edge tools, processes and skills for Atmanirbhar Bharat. IDEA Labs is a platform to experiment with ideas for qualitative change.

24. INNOVATION IN PEDAGOGY & ASSESSMENT TECHNIQUES FOR TECHNICAL EDUCATION

The National Education Policy (NEP) 2020, released by the Ministry of Education, emphasizes the need to transform the education system to make it more **student-centric, interdisciplinary, flexible, and inclusive.** The NEP 2020 envisions promoting **experiential and holistic learning that focuses on problem-solving, critical thinking, and innovation.** In line with this vision, Technical Education institutes must adapt and adopt advanced pedagogical methods and assessment techniques that cater to the diverse learning needs of students and promote active participation in the learning process. AICTE-IDEA (Idea Development, Evaluation & Application) Lab is one such successful initiative.

The All India Council for Technical Education (AICTE) and National Education Technology Forum (NETF) have been instrumental in promoting advanced pedagogical methods and assessment techniques in Technical Education institutes. They have been collaborating with universities, institutes, and other stakeholders to develop and implement innovative teaching and learning practices that ensure quality education. Their efforts have led to the introduction of new techniques such as **blended learning, flipped classrooms, project-based learning, case studies, simulations, and gamification**, to name a few.

Blended learning is a combination of online and face-to-face learning that allows students to learn at their own pace and convenience. It provides students with access to digital resources, including videos, online quizzes, interactive games, and simulations, which enhance the learning experience. Flipped classrooms, on the other hand, reverse the traditional learning model by having students watch lectures and learn the theory at home, while class time is used for problem-solving, group discussions, and practical application of concepts.

Ongoing efforts shall focus on promoting online learning alternatives such as SWAYAM and MOOCs and further their industry value through useful professional certifications relevant to Technical Education and with wide acceptance.

Project-based learning and Case Studies are another effective way of teaching technical subjects, where students work on real-world problems and apply the theoretical concepts they have learned to develop solutions. Simulations and gamification help make learning more engaging and interactive, as they create a virtual environment that simulates real-world scenarios.

Apart from advanced pedagogical methods, the assessment techniques must also evolve to align with the changing needs of Technical Education. The traditional examination-based approach is gradually being replaced by **formative and summative assessments that evaluate the students' understanding of the subject and their ability to apply it to real-world scenarios.**

National Digital Library of India (NDLI), a digital repository of learning resources that provides access to millions of books, journals, and research papers. The NDLI has made learning more accessible and has enabled students to learn at their own pace and convenience.

To promote and implement these advanced pedagogical methods and assessment techniques, Technical Education institutes must develop a strategy and an implementation plan that aligns with the NEP 2020. The strategy should focus on creating a student-centric and inclusive learning environment that caters to the diverse learning needs of students. It should also encourage interdisciplinary learning and promote the integration of technology in the teaching-learning process.

The implementation plan should involve faculty training programs that equip them with the necessary skills and knowledge to implement these advanced pedagogical methods and assessment techniques effectively. The plan should also involve the establishment of quality assurance mechanisms that ensure the continuous evaluation and improvement of the teaching-learning process.

25. ENABLING ENTREPRENEURIAL MINDSET THROUGH TECHNICAL EDUCATION

In today's fast-paced world, where technological advancements are disrupting every industry, it is imperative for educational institutions to equip students with the necessary skills to thrive in the dynamic landscape. Technical Education has always been a crucial component of the education system, as it prepares students for careers in fields such as engineering, information technology, and biotechnology. However, it is equally important to instil an entrepreneurial mindset in students, which can lead to the creation of innovative products and services and drive economic growth.

The National Education Policy (NEP) 2020 emphasizes the need to nurture an entrepreneurial spirit among students and create an ecosystem that supports innovation and entrepreneurship. The All India Council for Technical Education (AICTE) and the National Education Technology Forum (NETF) have taken various initiatives to enable an entrepreneurial mindset through Technical Education.

The NETF has proposed the **creation of a "sandbox" for entrepreneurs to test their education-based products or services.** This sandbox will provide a safe environment for students to experiment and develop their ideas without fear of failure. Additionally, it will offer access to resources, mentors, and funding opportunities, which are essential for the success of any start-up.

The AICTE has established an **Innovation Council** to promote innovation and entrepreneurship among students. The council has initiated several programs, such as the **Smart India Hackathon**, which encourages students to develop innovative solutions to real-world problems. The council also provides funding and mentorship to start-ups through its Start-up Policy.

To enable an entrepreneurial mindset, it is essential to provide students with the necessary skills and knowledge. The NEP 2020 emphasizes the need for experiential learning and hands-on training, which can help students develop practical skills and gain industry exposure. Technical Education institution should incorporate **project-based learning, internships, and apprenticeships** to provide students with real-world experience.

Furthermore, Technical Education institutions

should also offer courses in entrepreneurship and innovation to equip students with the necessary knowledge to start and run a successful business. These courses should cover topics such as **ideation, product development, marketing, finance, and business strategy.**

To enable entrepreneurship, it is also essential to create an ecosystem that supports innovation and start-ups. Technical Education institutions should **establish incubation centers and accelerators to provide resources and support to start-ups.** These centers should offer **mentorship, funding, legal assistance, and networking opportunities** to budding entrepreneurs. Also, to promote entrepreneurship, Student startups in domain will be encouraged to earn credits.

Enabling an entrepreneurial mindset through Technical Education is crucial for creating the next generation of innovators and job creators. The NEP 2020 and initiatives by AICTE have laid the foundation for fostering entrepreneurship in the education system.

Technical Education institutions should incorporate experiential learning, hands-on training, entrepreneurship courses, and establish incubation centers and accelerators to create an ecosystem that supports innovation and entrepreneurship.

AICTE promote the efforts of working with government agencies, industry associations, and financial institutions to create a supportive ecosystem for startups. The objective is to advocate for policies that encourage entrepreneurship, statutory -tax incentives, grants and other streamlined regulatory processes.

Going forward, there should be continuous Learning and Adaptation by recognizing the dynamic entrepreneurial landscape and fine tuning of curriculum reflecting the emerging trends and technologies. There must be encouragement for lifelong learning and provide resources for alumni to stay connected and engaged in the entrepreneurial community. Institutions should implement metrics to assess the impact of entrepreneurial programs on students' success, startup creation, and innovation and give credits, celebrate and showcase success stories to inspire current and future students, creating a culture that values and promotes entrepreneurship.

26. THE ROLE OF MENTORSHIP AND CAREER GUIDANCE IN TECHNICAL EDUCATION

In today's dynamic and rapidly changing world, students are faced with a plethora of career options, making it crucial to provide them with the right guidance and support to make informed decisions. In the realm of Technical Education, mentorship and career guidance can play a significant role in shaping the careers of aspiring engineers and technologists.

Under the National Education Policy 2020, the All India Council for Technical Education (AICTE) has emphasized the importance of mentorship and career guidance in Technical Education. The policy recognizes that students need guidance and mentorship to navigate the complex and ever-changing landscape of the job market.

To implement this policy, the AICTE has formulated a comprehensive strategy that includes,

- **Establishment of mentorship and career guidance cells in technical institutions.** These cells will be responsible for providing students with personalized guidance and support in making informed career choices.
- Developing a **network of mentors and experts** from various fields who can provide students with industry insights and mentorship. This network will be built through collaborations with industry associations, professional bodies, and alumni networks.
- Integrating technology-based solutions such as **chatbots and virtual mentors** into the mentorship and career guidance cells. These solutions will provide students with round-the-clock support and enable them to connect with mentors and experts from anywhere in the world.
- Development of a **Training program for mentors and career guidance professionals.** The program will focus on enhancing the skills of these professionals in providing personalized guidance to students and enabling them to keep up with the latest trends and developments in the job market.

Mentorship and career guidance are essential components of Technical Education that can play a critical role in shaping the careers of aspiring engineers and technologists. With the comprehensive strategy and implementation plan formulated by the AICTE, students can look forward to receiving personalized guidance and support to make informed career choices and navigate the complexities of the job market.

AICTE advocates the role of teachers as mentors and believes that each faculty is a change agent to mould upcoming generations. A teacher as a mentor is dedicated to following activities:

- Continuous updation on advanced Mentoring Skills
- Updating latest domain industry trends
- Fine tuning Professional Communication, Listening and giving Constructive Feedback to mentees
- Understanding mentoring, counselling and coaching roles
- Refer cases to experts at the right time to right persons
- Enhance evaluation, feedback and documentation procedures
- Sharing best practices through well connected network
- Ensuring results are reaching to all stakeholders
- Attain value added contribution to community and society

AICTE Mentor – Mentee Scheme (both on Margdarshan and IIC - Institute Innovation Council) focus on:

- Overall wellbeing and holistic development of students
- Faculty development to undertake mentoring, coaching and guidance roles
- Accountability by institution's management to integrate mentoring scheme to the curriculum and academic framework
- Real world insights and career guidance by Alumni
- Implementation through ERP
- Ensuring results are reaching to all stakeholders
- Review, Assessment and Analysis to measure the overall program impact.

27. DEVELOPING INSTITUTIONAL AUTONOMY FOR TECHNICAL EDUCATION IN INDIA

As India strives towards attaining its goal of becoming a global leader in Technical Education, there is a pressing need to address the issue of institutional autonomy. The National Education Policy 2020 has laid out a roadmap for transforming the education system in the country, including the Technical Education sector. The All India Council for Technical Education (AICTE) has been tasked with implementing these changes, which include promoting institutional autonomy.

Institutional autonomy is crucial for the growth and development of Technical Education institutions in India. It provides them with the **freedom to develop and implement their own curriculum, policies and procedures, and manage their finances.** This enables them to respond with agility to the changing needs of the industry and the market, and to provide their students with the best possible education.

The AICTE has recognized the importance of institutional autonomy, and has taken several steps to promote it. It has developed a strategy and implementation plan that includes creating an enabling environment for institutional autonomy, providing support and guidance to institutions, and building **a culture of self-assessment and accountability.**

One of the key elements of this strategy is the **establishment of a system of self-assessment and accreditation.** This will enable institutions to assess their own performance against pre-defined standards, and to identify areas for improvement. Accreditation will also provide a seal of quality that will enhance the reputation of the institution and increase its credibility.

Another important aspect of promoting institutional autonomy is the **provision of financial autonomy.** Institutions should be able to generate their own income and manage their finances without undue interference from external bodies. This will enable them to invest in the development of their infrastructure, faculty, and curriculum, and to provide their students with the best possible education.

The AICTE has also recognized the importance of promoting innovation and entrepreneurship in Technical Education. It has launched several initiatives aimed at encouraging institutions to develop their own innovative solutions and to support their students in becoming entrepreneurs. These initiatives include setting up innovation hubs and incubation centers, providing mentorship and support to aspiring entrepreneurs, and promoting collaboration between industry and academia.

Institutional autonomy is crucial for the growth and development of Technical Education in India. The AICTE has recognized its importance and has taken several steps to promote it. The implementation of these steps will enable institutions to respond to the changing needs of the industry and the market, and to provide their students with the best possible education.

28. THE NEED FOR MULTI-SECTORAL PARTNERSHIPS FOR TECHNICAL EDUCATION

In the current era of globalization, there is an increasing demand for highly skilled technical professionals who can drive innovation and economic growth. However, the task of producing such professionals cannot be accomplished by educational institutions alone. The need of the hour are multi-sectoral partnership that involves collaboration between academia, industry, government, and civil society. This partnership is essential to provide students with the knowledge and skills required to meet the challenges of the rapidly changing technological landscape.

The National Education Policy 2020 has recognized the importance of multi- sectoral partnerships in promoting Technical Education in India. The All India Council for Technical Education (AICTE) has been entrusted with the responsibility of forging partnerships between institutions of Technical Education and industry. This is being done through various initiatives such as the National Education Technology Forum (NETF), which aims to promote collaboration between academia, industry, and government in the field of Technical Education.

The partnership between academia and industry is particularly important, as it provides students with **hands-on experience in real-world settings.** Industry partners can provide **internships and apprenticeships to students,** which help them gain practical knowledge and skills. Furthermore, industry experts can also be invited to deliver **expert talks and guest lectures,** which expose students to the latest trends and developments in their respective fields.

Apart from academia and industry, government and civil society also have a crucial role to play in promoting Technical Education. The government can provide funding and other resources to educational institutions to **develop state-of-the-art infrastructure and facilities.** Civil society organizations can also play a key role by **providing mentorship and career guidance** to students.

The need for multi-sectoral partnerships in Technical Education cannot be overemphasized. A concerted effort by academia, industry, government, and civil society is required to produce the next generation of highly skilled technical professionals who can drive innovation and economic growth. The National Education Policy 2020 and the initiatives taken by AICTE provide a framework for such partnerships, and it is up to all stakeholders to work together towards this common goal.

29. BUILDING A CULTURE OF RESEARCH AND INNOVATION IN TECHNICAL EDUCATION INSTITUTIONS

Technical Education institutions play a crucial role in shaping the future of the country. They are responsible for producing skilled professionals who are well-equipped to tackle the challenges of the modern world. In recent times, there has been a growing emphasis on building a culture of research and innovation in these institutions. This vision document delves into the importance of research and innovation in Technical Education institutions and outlines a strategy and implementation plan for building a culture of research and innovation in these institutions.

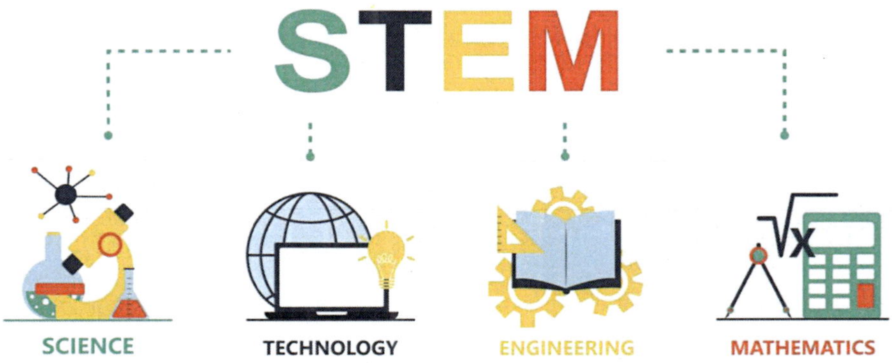

Research and innovation are essential components of Technical Education. They help institutions stay relevant and up-to-date with the latest advancements in technology. Moreover, they provide students with hands-on experience, which is crucial for their future careers. In addition, research and innovation also contribute to the development of new technologies and products, which can have a significant impact on the economy.

The National Education Policy 2020 emphasizes the need for research and innovation in Technical Education institutions. It states that institutions should focus on developing new technologies, products, and processes that are socially relevant and economically viable. Moreover, the policy calls for the establishment of research parks and incubation centers to foster research and innovation.

Strategy for Building a Culture of Research and Innovation

The following is a strategy for building a culture of research and innovation in Technical Education institutions:

- **Encourage Faculty to Engage in Research:** Institutions should encourage their faculty members to engage in research. They should provide them with incentives such as funding, sabbaticals, and recognition for their work. Moreover, they should create an environment that is conducive to research.

- **Promote Industry-Academia Collaboration:** Institutions should establish partnerships with the industry to promote collaboration between academia and industry. This collaboration can lead to the development of new technologies and products that are relevant to society. Industries may require specific research outcomes to address their practical problems or develop innovative solutions and faculties must be encouraged to take up such projects.

- **Establish Research Parks and Incubation Centers:** Research parks and incubation centers can provide a platform for students and faculty to work on research projects. They can also serve as a bridge between academia and industry, facilitating collaboration and knowledge transfer.

- **Foster Entrepreneurship:** Institutions should foster entrepreneurship by providing students with training in entrepreneurship and business management. They should also establish incubation centers to support start-ups.

- **Provide Access to State-of-the-Art Facilities:** Institutions should provide access to state-of-the-art facilities such as labs, equipment, and software to their faculty and students. This will enable them to conduct research in cutting-edge technologies.

Implementation Plan:

The following is an implementation plan for building a culture of research and innovation in Technical Education institutions:

- **Develop a Research Policy:** Institutions should develop a research policy that outlines the institution's goals and objectives for research. This policy should also specify the funding, incentives, and support that the institution will provide to its faculty members for research.

- **Establish Partnerships with Industry:** Institutions should establish partnerships with the industry to promote collaboration between academia and industry. These partnerships can be established through MoUs or joint projects.

- **Establish Research Parks and Incubation Centers:** Institutions should establish research parks and incubation centers to provide a platform for students and faculty to work on research projects. These centers can also provide support for start-ups.

- **Provide Training in Entrepreneurship:** Institutions should provide training in entrepreneurship and business management to their students. This can be done through workshops, seminars, and internships.

- **Provide Access to State-of-the-Art Facilities:** Institutions should provide access to state-of-the-art facilities such as labs, equipment, and software to their faculty and students. This can be achieved through the acquisition of new equipment and the development of partnerships with other institutions. **The Indian Science, Technology, and Engineering Facilities Map (I-STEM)** is one such initiative. It is a dynamic, interactive, user-friendly, indigenously web portal for shaping Science Research in India to achieve the Goal "Self-Reliant India". I-STEM holds the database of publically funded functioning R&D Equipment and Facilities in various public and private Institutions in India.

Research and innovation are essential components of Technical Education institutions. They have and shall continue to play a crucial role in the development of new technologies, products, and processes.

30. ADDRESSING THE CHALLENGES OF RURAL TECHNICAL EDUCATION IN INDIA

In India, one of the biggest challenges in the field of Technical Education is the issue of **providing quality education in rural areas.** While urban centers have access to advanced infrastructure and resources, rural areas often lack basic amenities necessary for the proper delivery of Technical Education. This has resulted in a significant disparity in the quality of Technical Education between urban and rural areas.

The National Education Policy 2020 recognizes the need to bridge this gap and has laid down specific guidelines to address this issue. The All India Council for Technical Education (AICTE) has been tasked with formulating a strategy and implementation plan to ensure that rural areas receive quality Technical Education.

The strategy involves **providing access to advanced infrastructure and resources, such as well-equipped labs, modern technology, and experienced faculty members.** AICTE has collaborated with various public and private sector entities to provide technical assistance, funding, and support for the development of rural Technical Education.

The implementation plan includes the **establishment of new Technical Education institutions in rural areas and upgrading the existing ones.** It also involves providing vocational training programs to equip students with practical skills required for employment. The AICTE has also encouraged institutions to adopt innovative teaching methodologies that cater to the specific needs of rural students.

The challenges in rural Technical Education are complex, and the solution requires a **multi-sectoral partnership approach.** This involves the involvement of local government bodies, NGOs, private sector organizations, and educational institutions. These partnerships can provide the necessary funding, infrastructure, and expertise to develop rural Technical Education. Furthermore, leveraging digital platforms can play a critical role in providing access to education in remote areas. AICTE has launched various initiatives, including the **National Education Alliance for Remote Areas (NEARA) and the APAAR (Automated Permanent Academic Account Registry)**, to promote online learning and increase access to Technical Education in rural areas.

The development of rural Technical Education is a crucial aspect of India's growth and progress. By addressing the challenges and implementing effective strategies, India can bridge the gap in Technical Education and provide equal opportunities to all students. The AICTE's efforts to provide infrastructure, training, and support to rural institutions will help India achieve its goal of becoming a global leader in Technical Education.

SWAYAM is one such initiative of **AICTE** which promotes education in rural areas. SWAYAM (Study Webs of Active-Learning for Young Aspiring Minds) MOOC Platform, was developed indigenously by AICTE in 2016 to facilitate hosting of online courses which can be accessed by anyone, anywhere at any time free of cost to achieve three cardinal principles of Education Policy viz. access, equity and quality. SWAYAM as one of the World's biggest Massive Open Online Courses (MOOCs) integrated platform of free online courses, cover subjects from high school onwards till higher education including Skill based courses to ensure that every student benefit from learning material through ICT.

31. IMPORTANCE OF FINANCIAL AID AND SCHOLARSHIPS IN TECHNICAL EDUCATION

As the world becomes increasingly competitive, it is more important than ever to ensure that everyone has access to quality education. Technical Education, in particular, has become an essential component of economic growth, and it is essential to provide financial aid and scholarships to ensure that everyone has equal access to these opportunities.

The National Education Policy 2020 has laid down a roadmap for India to become a knowledge-based economy. In order to achieve this goal, it is imperative that the country invests in its human capital by making Technical Education more accessible to all. The All India Council for Technical Education (AICTE) has a crucial role to play in this regard. The council has taken several measures to ensure that Technical Education is available to everyone, regardless of their financial situation.

One of the most significant steps taken by the AICTE has been to **introduce scholarships for students pursuing Technical Education.** These scholarships provide financial aid to students who may not be able to afford the cost of their education. In addition, the AICTE has also **encouraged institutions to offer financial aid to students who demonstrate academic excellence.** This has created a culture of competition among students and has also helped to ensure that the most deserving students receive financial aid.

Another way that the AICTE has supported Technical Education is by creating a **dedicated fund for economically weaker sections of society.** This fund provides financial assistance to students who come from low-income families and may not be able to afford the cost of their education. The AICTE has also created a mechanism for institutions to access this fund, making it easier for them to offer financial aid to students who need it.

The AICTE has also introduced schemes such as the **Pragati and Saksham schemes,** which aim to provide financial assistance to female and differently-abled students, respectively. These schemes provide financial assistance for tuition fees, hostel fees, and other related expenses, thereby making Technical Education more accessible to these groups.

Prime Minister's Special Scholarship Scheme (PMSSS) is a transformative scheme implemented by All India Council for Technical Education (AICTE) for the students of the UTs of J&K and Ladakh. The objective of the Scheme is to build up capacities in youth of J&K, educate, enable and empowering them to compete in normal course, thereby enhancing and boosting employment potentials for the students of J&K and Ladakh.

In addition to scholarships and financial aid, the AICTE has also taken several other measures to make Technical Education more affordable. For instance, the council has encouraged institutions to **offer flexible payment plans, so that students can pay their fees in instalments rather than upfront.** This has made it easier for students to manage their finances and has also reduced the burden of paying for education all at once.

The AICTE has also introduced a number of measures to improve the quality of Technical Education in the country. The council has set up a **system for accreditation of technical institutions, which ensures that only those institutions that meet certain quality standards are allowed to offer Technical Education.** This has helped to weed out institutions that do not provide quality education, thereby improving the overall quality of Technical Education in the country.

Financial aid and scholarships are essential for ensuring that everyone has equal access to quality Technical Education. The AICTE has taken several measures to ensure that Technical Education is accessible to all, including those from economically weaker sections of society. By providing scholarships, creating dedicated funds for low-income students, and encouraging institutions to offer flexible payment plans, the AICTE has made Technical Education more affordable for everyone. These measures have not only increased access to Technical Education but have also improved the quality of education offered in the country.

32. ADDRESSING NEEDS OF DIFFERENTLY ABLED STUDENTS IN TECHNICAL EDUCATION

In recent times, there has been an increasing focus on creating an inclusive and equitable education system that caters to the diverse needs of students. Technical Education institutions are no exception to this, and it is important to ensure that differently-abled students are provided with equal opportunities to pursue their academic interests and achieve their full potential.

The National Education Policy 2020 recognizes the importance of providing accessible education to all students, irrespective of their background or ability. The policy emphasizes the need to create a supportive and inclusive learning environment that caters to the needs of all students, including differently-abled ones. The All India Council for Technical Education (AICTE) has also laid down guidelines and regulations to ensure that technical institutions provide necessary facilities and accommodations to differently- abled students.

Despite these efforts, there are still several challenges that need to be addressed to ensure that differently-abled students are able to fully participate in Technical Education. One of the primary challenges is the **lack of infrastructure and facilities that cater to the needs of differently-abled students.** Technical institutions need to provide accessible classrooms, laboratories, libraries, and other facilities that are **equipped with assistive technologies and tools to aid learning.**

Another challenge is the **lack of awareness and sensitization among faculty and staff** towards the needs of differently-abled students. It is important to provide training and development programs to faculty and staff to help them understand the needs of differently-abled students and provide appropriate support and accommodations.

In addition, financial barriers can also hinder the participation of differently- abled students in Technical Education. **Scholarships and financial aid programs** can help alleviate the financial burden on students and provide them with the necessary resources to pursue their academic interests. Technical institutions should work towards providing scholarships and financial aid to differently-abled students to ensure that they are not excluded from pursuing Technical Education due to financial constraints.

Furthermore, it is important to create a supportive and inclusive culture within technical institutions that fosters the participation and success of differently-abled students. This can be achieved by creating **student support services that provide counselling, mentoring, and guidance to differently-abled students.** In addition, creating peer support networks and student organizations can help build a sense of community and belonging among differently-abled students.

To address these challenges, technical institutions need to develop a comprehensive strategy and implementation plan that prioritizes the needs of differently-abled students. This plan should focus on creating accessible infrastructure and facilities, providing appropriate support and accommodations, sensitizing faculty and staff towards the needs of differently-abled students, providing financial aid and scholarships, and creating a supportive and inclusive culture within the institution.

It is crucial to address the needs of differently-abled students in Technical Education to ensure that they are provided with equal opportunities to pursue their academic interests and achieve their full potential. Technical institutions should work towards creating a supportive and inclusive learning environment that caters to the diverse needs of all students, including differently-abled ones. This can be achieved through a comprehensive strategy and implementation plan that prioritizes the needs of differently- abled students and ensures that they are not excluded from pursuing Technical Education due to physical, financial, or other barriers.

33. IMPORTANCE OF SOFT SKILLS & HIGHER ORDER THINKING SKILLS

In today's rapidly evolving job market, Technical Education graduates need to possess more than just technical skills to be successful. Employers are now seeking candidates who possess a wide range of **soft skills, including critical thinking, problem-solving, lifelong learning,** and experiential learning. In this regard, Technical Education institutions must equip their students with the necessary skills to be employable. The National Education Policy 2020, which provides a comprehensive framework for the development of education in India, recognizes the importance of soft skills and has **emphasized the need to develop a broad-based and multidisciplinary education system.** To achieve this objective, the All India Council for Technical Education (AICTE) has introduced the National Education Technology Forum (NETF) to promote the use of technology in education, including the development of e- content, online teaching-learning processes, and online assessments.

The AICTE has also recommended various measures to enhance the soft skills of Technical Education graduates, including **the incorporation of critical thinking and problem-solving skills in the curriculum.** This can be achieved through the development of experiential learning programs that provide students with hands-on experience in real-world scenarios.

Importance of Soft Skills:

Soft skills are becoming increasingly important in the workforce. Employers are looking for candidates who can communicate effectively, work well in teams, and possess leadership qualities. In technical fields, it is essential that graduates possess these skills to effectively collaborate with colleagues, communicate with clients, and lead teams. Soft skills can be developed through various activities such as group projects, public speaking, and internships.

Critical Thinking and Problem Solving:

Technical Education graduates must be able to think critically and solve complex problems. This is especially important in fields such as engineering and computer science, where problem-solving skills are crucial. Critical thinking skills are developed through rigorous coursework, projects, and internships. By analysing real-world problems, students learn how to apply their technical knowledge to real- world situations and develop solutions that are both effective and efficient.

Lifelong Learning:

The modern job market is constantly evolving, and it is important that Technical Education graduates continue to learn throughout their careers. Lifelong learning is essential in ensuring that graduates remain relevant in their fields and can adapt to new technologies and work environments. Technical Education institutions must promote a culture of lifelong learning by providing access to resources such as online courses and workshops.

Experiential Learning:

Experiential learning is a crucial component of Technical Education. By engaging in hands-on activities, students gain practical experience and develop skills that are essential in the workforce. Technical Education institutions should provide opportunities for students to engage in experiential learning activities such as internships, research projects, and fieldwork.

AICTE has also emphasized the need for lifelong learning, which involves the continuous development of skills and knowledge throughout an individual's career. To promote this, Technical Education institutions can provide students with access to online learning resources and encourage them to participate in continuing education programs. Another essential aspect is the development of communication skills, teamwork, and leadership skills, which are necessary for success in the workplace. Technical Education institutions can incorporate **group projects, presentations, and internships** to develop these skills among their students.

The employability of Technical Education graduates depends on their possession of soft skills in addition to technical skills. The National Education Policy 2020 and the AICTE recognize the importance of soft skills and have taken measures to enhance them. Technical Education institutions must incorporate experiential learning, promote lifelong learning, and develop communication, teamwork, and leadership skills to ensure their students' success in the job market.

34. ADDRESSING THE CHALLENGES OF ONLINE AND HYBRID TECHNICAL EDUCATION

Amid the ongoing pandemic, online and hybrid Technical Education has become an increasingly important topic in the education sector. The advent of technology has presented both opportunities and challenges for students pursuing Technical Education. While online and hybrid education provides flexibility and accessibility, it also poses unique challenges that must be addressed.

The National Education Policy 2020 and the AICTE have recognized the significance of online and hybrid education and are working towards developing strategies to enhance the quality of Technical Education provided through these modes. The **NETF sandbox for entrepreneurs** to test their education-based products or services can also play a crucial role in the development and implementation of these strategies.

However, there are several challenges that must be addressed to ensure that online and hybrid Technical Education is effective and inclusive.

- Technical courses are often hands-on and require access to specialized equipment and labs, which may not be readily available in an online setting.
- The lack of face-to-face interaction between instructors and students can hinder the development of critical skills, such as problem-solving and communication.
- Students from rural areas and economically weaker sections may not have access to the necessary technology and internet connectivity required for online and hybrid education. These issues can lead to a lack of motivation and engagement, which can ultimately impact the employability of Technical Education graduates.

To address these challenges, the AICTE and other stakeholders must work towards developing comprehensive strategies that **integrate hands-on learning experiences and soft skills development into online and hybrid Technical Education.** These strategies must also focus on providing financial

assistance and support for students from marginalized backgrounds, such as differently-abled students and those from economically weaker sections.

Furthermore, the AICTE must collaborate with industry partners to provide access to **specialized equipment and labs, as well as opportunities for internships and apprenticeships.** This will help bridge the gap between theoretical knowledge and practical application, and enhance the employability of Technical Education graduates.

Online and hybrid Technical Education presents both opportunities and challenges that must be addressed to ensure its effectiveness and inclusivity. Through collaborative efforts and comprehensive strategies, the AICTE and other stakeholders can create a more equitable and accessible Technical Education system that prepares graduates for success in the ever-evolving job market.

National Educational Alliance for Technology (NEAT) cell at AICTE offers wide range of courses in collaboration with many private industries. The aim of NEAT is to bring the best technological Products in education pedagogy on a single platform for the convenience of learners.

Likewise, 'Study Webs of Active Learning for Young Aspiring Minds' **(SWAYAM)**, also provides one integrated platform and MOOCs (Massive Open Online Courses) portal for online courses, using Information and Communication Technology (ICT) and covering all higher education subjects and skill sector courses. All the courses are interactive, prepared by the best teachers in the country like IIT/NIT Professors and are available, free of cost.

35. EFFECTIVE MONITORING & EVALUATION FRAMEWORK FOR 2047 STRATEGY

In order to ensure the effective monitoring and evaluation of the success of the vision, plan, and strategy for Technical Education by 2047, there is a pressing need for a robust and comprehensive framework that can provide a clear roadmap for the various stakeholders involved in this critical sector. The National Education Policy 2020, which was launched with much fanfare and anticipation, has laid out an ambitious vision for the future of Technical Education in India. However, in order to turn this vision into a reality, it is essential to have a detailed plan of action that can guide the various initiatives and interventions that are required. The All India Council for Technical Education (AICTE), which is the apex regulatory body for Technical Education in the country, has an important role to play in this regard. The AICTE has already launched several initiatives and programs aimed at promoting excellence in Technical Education, such as the **National Employability Enhancement Mission (NEEM) and the Startup Policy Framework.** However, in order to ensure that these initiatives are effective and achieve their intended objectives, it is important to have a robust monitoring and evaluation framework in place.

One of the key challenges in this regard is to **develop appropriate metrics and indicators that can capture the complex and multifaceted nature of Technical Education.** This requires a deep understanding of the various components that contribute to the success of Technical Education, such as **infrastructure, faculty quality, curriculum design, industry-academia linkages, and research and innovation.** Moreover, it is important to take into account the diverse and evolving needs of different stakeholders, including students, faculty, industry, and policymakers.

To address these challenges, it is essential to **develop a collaborative and participatory monitoring and evaluation framework** that can involve all the relevant stakeholders. This can be achieved through the establishment of a national-level task force or committee that can oversee the implementation of the Technical Education vision and plan. This task force can comprise representatives from the AICTE, the Ministry of Education, industry associations, academic institutions, and student organizations, among others. The task force can,

- Develop appropriate metric s and indicators for monitoring and evaluating the various initiatives and interventions.
- Facilitate the sharing of best practices and lessons learned across different institutions and regions.
- Ensure that the Technical Education vision and plan remains aligned with the changing needs and priorities of the country.

Effective monitoring and evaluation of the success of the vision, plan, and strategy for Technical Education by 2047 requires a collaborative and participatory approach that involves all the relevant stakeholders. This requires the development of appropriate metrics and indicators that can capture the complex and multifaceted nature of Technical Education. It also requires the establishment of a national-level task force or committee that can oversee the implementation of the Technical Education vision and plan, and ensure its alignment with the changing needs and priorities of the country. By taking these steps, India can build a world-class Technical Education system that can contribute to the country's growth and development in the years to come.

By taking these steps, India can build a world-class Technical Education system that can contribute to the country's growth and development in the years to come. These proactive steps will play a pivotal role in Viksit Bharat and making India a hub of technical education by 2047.

36. 2047 TECHNICAL EDUCATION ACTION PLAN

2047, is not mere a year for India but a transformative turn to revamp the status of Developing India to a Developed India. The vision of Viksit Bharat @2047 encompasses various aspects of development but the culture of start-ups and entrepreneurship is one of the main aspect to make India stand tall globally. To instil the future generation with the entrepreneurial capability, the role of Technical Education is significant. By 2047, India aims to be a hub of Technical Education and in order to achieve this, a systematic approach is the key. The following strategic vision is chalked out in three phases to make India technically strong and Vikist by 2047:

2047 Technical Education Action Plan		
Vision 2047 - Technical Education		
Phase	**Theme**	**Areas of Focus: Quality | Equality | Accessibility | Affordability | Accountability**
Phase-I 2028	Sowing Seeds of Change	• Promoting Utilization of Digital / Online Learning Pedagogical approaches focused on learning outcomes (SWAYAM, NEAT, DigitalSkilling) • Curriculum Reform and Alignment to Industry requirements (NCFHE) • Promoting Vocational Education, Industry exposure and OJT practical learning through Internships and Apprenticeships embedded into technical education curriculum (NIP, NATS) • Establishing new technical institutions in underserved regions • Establishing Centres of Excellence in emerging technologies' such as AI/ML, Robotics, and Quantum Computing etc. • Concerted efforts towards streamlining Faculty Development Programs and targeted Career Progression Frameworks for Teachers (APAAR) • Establishing a culture of research, innovation and product development as part of technical education curricula (National Research Foundation, Incubation Centres, Atal Innovation Mission, Startup India Program) • Restructuring monitoring framework to achieve globally benchmarked Accreditation and Quality Review of Technical Institutions (HECI, ONOD) • Establishing centralized collection of Technical Education data for centralized monitoring and control and ensuring authenticity of reported data and infrastructure (ONOD) • Promoting multilingual accessibility to quality education and tools to unlock youth potential uninhibited by language barriers (Anuvadini) • Driving multidisciplinary collaboration through dedicated Innovation and Entrepreneurship Development Centre (IEDC) in every technical institution

2047 Technical Education Action Plan

Vision 2047 - Technical Education

Phase	Theme	Areas of Focus: Quality | Equality | Accessibility | Affordability | Accountability
Phase - II 2038	Nurturing Saplings of Growth	• Universal acceptance of NDEAR Digital Open Architecture based online education platforms with seamless user experience and mobility (NETF) • Driving Ecosystem innovation in experiential and holistic learning through open and integrated Sandbox Environments • Driving personalized and customized learning pathways through AI/ ML recommendation engines • Use of AI/ML for proliferating IoT based Smart Classrooms in Technical Educations • Pedagogical Innovations in Machine Assisted Learning through virtual mentors, chatbots • Immutable Blockchain based Registry of Students, Teachers that shall track cumulative academic and skilling credentials while empowering users with control over their own data • Establishment of National Accreditation Council for conducting assessment of technical educational institutions on aspects of learning outcomes, teaching quality and research. • Promoting Internationalization of Indian Technical Education and manifesting a global brand of quality and affordable technical educational opportunities (Study in India) • Implementation of Mentor – Mentee Scheme • Implementation of AICTE SLA PARAKH system • Using data driven policy decision making to compensate for regional student aspirations and creating suitable pathways for success in their professional careers (ONOD + APAAR)
Phase-III 2047	**Extending Benefits of Ecosystem Innovation**	• Complete Digitalization of Technical Education resources with multiple models of consumption – hybrid/online with expansion of Virtual Reality and Augmented Reality based pedagogical structures • Utilization of AI Virtual Teaching Assistants for significant part of curriculum and the embracing of the role of mentor by teachers who imbibe higher order thinking skills and soft skills to students in order to succeed in their professional careers.

37. VARIOUS INITIATIVES OF AICTE FOR THE BETTERMENT OF STUDENTS, FACULTY & INSTITUTIONS

The All India Council for Technical Education (AICTE) is playing a pivotal role in shaping the landscape of technical education in India. Since 2014, under the government's thrust on improving the quality and relevance of technical skills, the Council prepared a perspective plan for technical education by involving industry bodies. AICTE has taken various initiatives and making concerted efforts to implement NEP-2020 in letter and spirit. Major highlights are as follows:

I. Student Centric Education:

1. Focus on Quality Assurance:

- **Revision of curriculum** with multidisciplinary approach to align with the provisions of NEP 2020 & Industry needs.
- **Implementation of National Curriculum & Credit Framework** to facilitate multiple entry/exit provisions, integration of vocational education with STEM education in line with NEP 2020.
- **Inclusion of BCA & BBA/BBM** offered through General Degree Colleges (Non-Technical Institutions) under the ambit of AICTE to ensure quality and coordinated, structured development of technical and management education.
- **Model Curricula for 9- new emerging technologies** such as Artificial Intelligence, Data Science etc. developed.
- **Flexibility in eligibility criteria for admission** to undergraduate Engineering and Technology programmes in line with NEP. Broadening the entry level qualifications; provide 14 subjects as possible options for admission to engineering. Provision for bridge courses by the institutions; to enhance subject specific knowledge.
- **New B.Tech Programmes** in VLSI Design Tech, Logistic & Supply Chain management, Data Science and Artificial Intelligence, and Diploma in IC Manufacturing launched to meet the growing manpower requirement in these areas. Enhanced focus on student learning outcomes and employability skills.
- **AICTE's Students Learning Assessment (PARAKH)** portal promotes holistic assessment of faculty and students' learning outcomes. 1.28 Lakh multiple-choice questions have been uploaded incorporating multiple disciplines towards improving the overall competence of students & graduates to include core disciplines, aptitude, emerging areas and higher order thinking skills.
- **Holistic Education: 3-week Mandatory Student Induction Program (SIP)** for a smooth transition from school, preparation for an environment for higher education which includes- (UHV-I Module: 15 sessions introductory UHV-I, 6 IKS Modules: includes Holistic Health and 2-Skill Modules).

Registration on AICTE-Student Learning Assessment Portal during 2023-24

(Current Status * Till 4th Dec,2023)

Institute Registered	Students Registered	Assessment Took by students	Faculty Registered
4347	6,58,491	4,40,993	40,792

(*Out of 7879 eligible institutes for PARAKH Assessment 4347 Institutes have registered).

Scholarship Schemes

Providing financial support to students from diverse backgrounds

AICTE Pragati Scholarship Scheme for Girl Students:
Scholarship of Rs. 50,000/- per annum to meritorious girl students Total 10,000 scholarships (5000 for Diploma and 5000 for Degree).

AICTE Swanath Scholarship Scheme:
The Scheme is being implemented by AICTE provides scholarship of upto Rs. 50, 000/- to provide support to orphans, wards of parents died due to Covid-19, wards of Armed Forces and Central Paramilitary Forces martyred in action (Shaheed) to pursue

AICTE Saksham Scholarship Scheme for Differently-abled Students:
Scholarship of upto Rs. 50, 000/- per annum to differently abled (minimum 40%) students.

AICTE Post-Graduate (PG) Scholarship Scheme:
Scholarship of Rs.12400/- per month for 24 months to the students admittedin AICTE approved. Institutions /Programs and within approved Intake of M.E. / M. Tech./M. Arch./M. Des. who qualify the GATE/CEED exam as per the guidelines.

Prime Ministers Special Scholarship Scheme (PMSSS):
To provide academic fee and maintenance allowance to students belonging to J&K and Ladakh. Under the scheme 5000 fresh scholarships are available per annum for students who secure admission (after passing XII) in Government Colleges /Institutions outside the Uts of J&K and Ladakh.

2. Enhancing Access, Equity and Affordability;

(i) **Increased intake capacity:** Approving new technical institutions and programs, particularly in rural areas, to cater to rising demand. Today total intake capacity is 30,79,612 in 8264 AICTE Approved Institutions across the country.

Flexi-timing for working professionals:- Provision for employed persons to upgrade their academic qualification/skill sets at diploma/degree/ postgraduate level through flexible mode of teaching-learning. (timings).

(ii) **Promotion of Indian regional Languages in technical education (Linguistic inclusivity):**

AICTE has introduced up to 50% of sanctioned intake in Indian regional languages, with 51 engineering colleges offering 16 courses in 7 languages in the academic year 2022-23.

AICTE's AI-based translator tool 'Anuvadini' is translating technical books into Hindi, Marathi, Bengali, Tamil, Telugu, and Kannada, aiming to break language barriers and promote linguistic inclusivity. This initiative enhances Gross Enrolment Ratio, improves access, taps into regional talent, and fosters research and innovation in regional ecosystems.

(iii) **National Educational Alliance for Technology (NEAT)** is an initiative providing top Ed-tech solutions for youth employability, freely accessible to Socially and Economically Disadvantaged Groups (SEDGs). 58 Ed-Tech companies offering 100 products, addressing employable skills, capacity building, and learning gaps online. To date, 12 lakh NEAT free coupons worth Rs. 254 crores have been distributed to SEDGs, facilitating access to quality courses through the NEAT Portal. The NEAT 3.0 portal, with a focus on vocational, upskilling, and reskilling, has been launched to enhance skills and employability.

(iv) **Internship:** Through internship portal has created an impressive milestone with 1.7 crore students' registered on the portal, 28 lakh Internships Posted and 75000 Industries/ Companies on boarded for enhancing students' skills, employability opportunities and transforms them into Industry Suitable Workforce.

(v) **Skill Development:** AICTE's initiatives for imparting Skills and enhancement of Employability in Technical Education through Kaushal Augmentation and Reskilling Mission of AICTE (KARMA). Approx. 16,000 students were trained under the KARMA scheme in the year 2022. KARMA scheme of AICTE is providing National Skill Qualification Framework (NSQF) compliant industrial training to students. These are short term Training Programmes.

(vi) **Indian Knowledge System (IKS) Portal:** Established 53 IKS centers dedicated to research and promotion of IKS. Conducted 88 IKS research projects, contributing to the advancement of Indian knowledge and cultural understanding. Provided over 5200 IKS internships, offering valuable practical experience to students interested in IKS. Conducted training programs for 2500 teachers, empowering them to incorporate IKS into their curriculum and teaching practices. 400,000+ general public outreach.

Digitized more than 1800 books related to IKS in searchable formats for preserving valuable source-texts for future generations

(vii) Guidelines for Imparting technical education through ODL & Online mode: To streamline and regulate the technical education AICTE has framed guidelines and gazette notification has been issued in 2021 for according approval to technical institutions in the area of computer applications, data science & artificial intelligence, Logistics and Travel & Tourism. During the Academic Year 2021-22, the approved intake for offering courses under online mode is 94,670 and in ODL mode is 1, 31,570.

II. Faculty Centric initiatives:

(i) **Faculty Development Programme through AICTE Training and Learning (ATAL) Academy:** Imparted training to more than 3 lakh faculty members on emerging niche areas such as AI, IoT, ML, DL, AR/VR, Robotics, Block Chain Management etc. across 1900 FDPs. ATAL Academies are being established at Guwahati and Jaipur. The ATAL Academy has received prestigious awards for its outstanding contribution to faculty development.

(ii) **AICTE- National Initiative for Technical Teachers Training (AICTE-NITTT):** In order to train the Inductee Teachers in AICTE approved / recognised institutions, National Initiative for Technical Teachers Training (for Inductee Teachers) has been launched. It imparts training to the Inductee Teachers in three phases.

(iii) **AICTE-Doctoral Fellowship (NDF):** Since the academic year 2018-19, the AICTE's National Doctoral Fellowship (NDF) supports full-time Ph.D. students in 28 designated research institutes, offering a monthly fellowship of Rs. 31,000 (JRF) for the first two years, followed by Rs. 35,000 (SRF) with HRA as per government norms. Two new schemes under Research Promotion Scheme have been launched specifically for North-East Region and for National Doctoral Fellow Centers(NFC)

(iv) **Examination Reforms Policy** based on Outcome Based Education creates a shift from rote learning and encourages, complex problem-solving, critical thinking, creativity, people management, teamwork and collaboration, emotional intelligence, judgement and decision-making, project management and cognitive flexibility.

More than 10000 faculty members have been trained on AICTE's Examination Reforms Policy. A data bank of approx. 7,600 multiple questions and 1,300 subjective on core technical disciplines is available.

III. Institute Centric:

1. **Initiatives:**

(i) Margdarshak - Margdarshan Initiative (Mentor-mentee handholding among institutes) to enhance the overall quality of technical institutes. 44 Mentor Institutes (MIs) and 391 senior academicians serve as Margdarshaks, guiding and mentoring 894 Mentee Beneficiary Institutes (MBIs) striving for accreditation. This initiative has resulted in 126 institutes obtaining NBA accreditation, with 80 institutes submitting Self-Assessment Reports for accreditation consideration.

(ii) **Good Governance and Technology Integration for ease of doing business:** AICTE Approval process transformed from offline to online mode completely;

- Robust, transparent and credible online **e-governance system** for approval is in force.
- Trust based governance-Self-disclosure-based approval.
- DBT System for Scholarships, funds for faculty and students from offline to online mode which has brought complete transparency and accountability.
- e-Governance has brought

transparency, accountability, credibility and efficiency in day-to-day activities of the organization and resulted in getting two National Awards

(iii) **Provision for Extension of Approval up to 3 years** for outstanding Institutions has been made in Approval Process Handbook 2024-2027.

(iv) **Guidelines framed for Grant of Autonomy to Polytechnics** to promote excellence in Diploma Level Education in Polytechnics

(v) **Vidyanjali Higher Education Volunteer Programme** aimed at creating a Pool of volunteers to build academic, training, and infrastructure support for institutions in higher education.

VIDYANJALI HIGHER EDUCATION (data as on 19th May, 2023)	
On Boarded Higher Education Institutes	1003
Registered Volunteers	19383
Requests Posted	1001
Requests Accepted by volunteers	512

(vi) **Yuva Sangam** under **Ek Bharat Shreshtha Bharat(EBSB):** AICTE successfully conducted 3 phases of Yuva Sangam; 3767 students and 367 Coordinators participated in this programme in last 2-years.

2. Fostering Innovation and Entrepreneurship:

(i) **AICTE IDEA (Idea Development, Evaluation & Application) Lab Scheme:** AICTE- IDEA Labs with prototyping facilities being set-up in institutions with a view to fostering the culture of innovation and critical thinking through hands-on experience and learning by doing.

- 106 institutions across 22 states/UTs have been identified to establish AICTE-IDEA Labs.
- 2-ATAL IDEA Labs are being established by AICTE, in DCRUST- Murthal (Haryana) and VTU- Muddanhalli (Karnataka).

(ii) **MoE-Innovation Cell in AICTE in 2018:**

Since the establishment of Innovation Cell in Year 2018, a large number (more than 30) of new initiatives and schemes have been launched by Innovation Cell.

a) **Building a vibrant network of Institution's Innovation Councils (IICs) in HEIs:**

- Vibrant network of Institution's Innovation Councils (IICs) in more than 7600+ HEIs have been established
- **There are more than 14 sub programs are complementing and supplement the IIC structure to achieve the I&E mission.**

b) **Faculty Innovation Ambassador (IA) Training Program in HEIs;** 26000+ faculty members from HEIs have been trained and deployed as Innovation Ambassadors to drive campus I&E ecosystems in educational institutions.

c) **Mentor-Mentee Program for IIC;** 205 high performing IIC institutions are supported by MIC with grant support for their role as mentor and guiding 550 IIC institutions in improving their competencies.

d) **Impact Lecture (IL) Series Program for IIC Institutions** So far, 1200+ IIC institutions have been organized 3600+ impact lectures and 1800+ ecosystem enablers have been engaged.

e) **YUKTI –Innovation and IPR Repository** creation in each and every IIC institutions is another unique approach of AICTE and

MIC is to integrate a market convergence platform to build a system of repository of ideas, innovations and start-ups developed in academic institutions.

So far a repository of 99000+ ideas, innovations and start-ups have been created in 1500 IIC institutions and are acting as pipeline of quality innovations for incubation units for further handholding and market linkage support.

f) **The YUKTI Innovation Challenge 2023** for fostering collaboration among innovators, institutions, government agencies, and experts to enhance the campus ecosystem. Supported 5000+ innovations, with 75 receiving Rs. 10.00 lakhs each for venture initiation, and the current challenge involves mentoring 4000+ innovations, with the top 100-150 set to receive funding assistance from AICTE & MIC.

g) **IICs in HEIs Linkage with Atal Tinkering Labs (ATLs) in Schools for Mentorship Support:** Atal Tinkering Labs (ATLs) established in schools are being linked with nearby higher education institutions having Institution's Innovation Councils (IICs) at pan India level. So far more than 3000 ATLs are linked with 800 IICs and mentoring activities are in progress.

h) **Introduction of New Academic Program at PG Level and Model Curriculum on MBA/ PGDM in Innovation, Entrepreneurship and Venture Development (IEV):** As of 2022-23 there are 26 AICTE approved institutes are running this course.

i) **Introduction of New Academic Program at UG Level and Model Curriculum on Minor Degree in Innovation, Entrepreneurship and Venture Development (IEV).**

j) **Setting up INDOVATION Centres in Various Regions to Promote Technology Transfer and IP Commercialisation:** 12-13 Indovation centers in regional locations will be established to facilitate technology transfer, IP commercialization, innovation, and entrepreneurship development in higher educational institutions across the country.

k) **National and International Hackathons:** organising different editions of hackathons round the year such as Smart India Hackathons, Toycathons, Drug Discovery Hackathon, Manthan and numbers of International Hackathons like Singapore India Hackathon, Indian - ASEAN Hackathon, India-Africa Hackathon to trigger creative mind-sets among Indian youths and engaging them in solving national and international problems and nation building process.

l) **Adoption of National Innovation and Startup Policy (NISP) guidelines in HEIs:** So far, more than 3200+ higher education institutes (both technical and non-technical) have adopted the policy.

m) **Benchmarking I&E Ecosystem in HEIs through NIRF-Innovation (Atal Ranking of Institutions on Innovation Achievements):** The participation from both technical and non-technical HEIs have been increased substantially from 496 HEIs in very first edition of ARIIA (2019) to record high participation of 1438 HEIs for ARIIA 2021. For the ARIIA 2022, 1417 HEIs are part of the benchmarking process.

n) **Organizing Regional Meets for IIC Institutions.**

(iii) Global Outreach of Higher Education

a) **In the QIP scheme**, a semester-based learning to faculty members in foreign universities for pursuing Ph.D. is allowed now. AICTE – MITACS scheme providing opportunities for students to pursue Internships and Incubator support in Canada. Credit transfer for one semester student exchange program.

b) **SWAYAM-MOOCS Platform** launched to bridge digital divide; Students from 218 Countries have been accessing SWAYAM MOOCs courses.

c) **Provision for Supernumerary seats** for NRIs/OCIs and PIOs.

d) **Twinning Program** for collaboration with universities abroad. Provision has been made for Collaboration between Indian Institutions/ Universities and Foreign Institutions/ Universities through allowing Dual Degree and Joint Degree.

- e) **International Cell** has been set up to give boost to collaboration of Indian Institutions with Foreign Institutions to make India global hub of education

(iv) **Canada India Acceleration Program (CIAP)**

The Canada India Acceleration Program (CIAP) by AICTE is an international startup exchange initiative jointly implemented by AICTE and Carleton University and has successfully completed two cohorts, supporting 15 women entrepreneurs. These entrepreneurs were selected from various innovation competitions, and their projects focus on areas like affordable healthcare and environmental waste management. AICTE and MIC have provided funding support of up to Rs. 10 lakhs for technology development and startup incubation during the financial years 2020-21.

AICTE QUALITY INITIATIVES

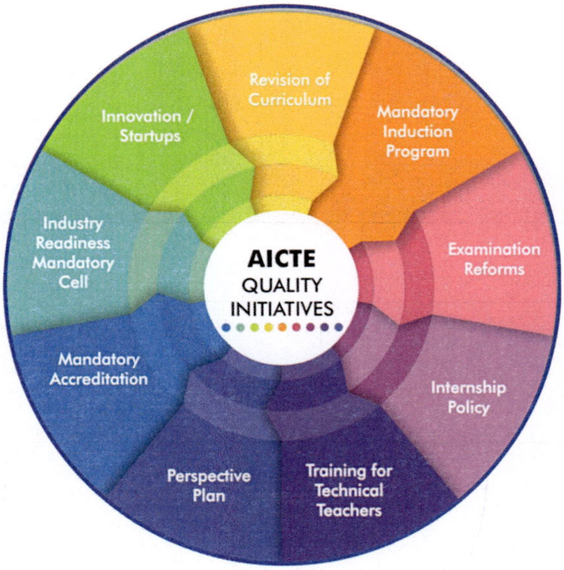

38. GLIMPSES OF AICTE ACTIVITIES IN 2023

1

Smart India Hackathon (SIH)

Prime Minister Shri Narendra Modi interacted with the participants of SIH. This year more than 50,000 ideas were submitted by 44,000 teams, marking a sevenfold jump from the first edition.

2

Launch of Placement Portal:

AICTE launched the 'AICTE Placement Portal' tailored for students residing in rural and tribal areas. More than 2,000 companies operating in different fields and segments have empanelled with the portal.

3

Launch of Margdarshan Scheme 2023-24

AICTE launched the Scheme with an aim to elevate the standard of technical education nationwide by providing dedicated ment-oring and guidance to Mentee Beneficiary Institutes (MBI) through the collaboration of Margdarshan Institutes (MI).

4

Courses for Working Professionals

AICTE allows working professionals to continue, complete or restart their higher education. AICTE has permitted ITI, diploma and undergraduate-working professionals to further upgrade their academic

5

Launch of AMRUT

AICTE launched "AMRUT - AICTE Millet Recipe Unleashing Talent" - a unique platform to showcase skills and passion for Millet-based dishes.

GLIMPSES OF AICTE ACTIVITIES

6

Introduction of Minor Degree Courses

AICTE introduced minor degree courses for core engineering students in subjects like semiconductor, integrated circuits, VLSI design, 5G Technology, AI etc. The initiative aims to enhance student's employability and broaden their knowledge base, making them better placed in the ever-changing job market.

7

One Student One Tree Campaign

The campaign was launched by AICTE to create awareness about Mission LiFE.

8

Women Entrepreneurship in Waste Management

AICTE inaugurated Women entrepreneurship in Waste Management (WEWP) Conclave 2023, amalgamating both these challenges of our Country and converting it into an opportunity to empower women as well as manage the waste in the country.

9

NICE 2023

AICTE with Ministry of Education and UGC organised the National Inter-College Cryptic Crossword Competition (NICE) for students as part of the Azadi Ka Amrit Mahotsav celebrations, aimed to promote ek bharat shrestha bharat.

10

Bicycle Design Challenge 2023

AICTE organised BCDC with a vision to encourage innovation and creativity in design and making of electric and non e-electric cycles, promote sustainable transportation and provide solutions to the challenges facing urban mobility in India.

GLIMPSES OF AICTE ACTIVITIES

11

One Student One Laptop:

AICTE introduced 'One Student One Laptop' (OSOL) initiative to make good use of technology in education for students in higher education institutions. The initiative aimed to enhance and explore digital learning, transform academic journey, revolutionize the ability of acquiring skills, foster creativity and critical thinking and equip students with ICT tools.

12

Inventors Challenge

The second edition of Inventors Challenge was jointly organised by AICTE, Arm Education and STMicroelectronics to develop the country's semiconductor ecosystem and catalyze India's rapidly expanding electronics manufacturing industry.

13

One Nation One Data:

The establishment of ONOD portal will allow sharing of regulatory HEI data reporting between various stakeholders through a network of Open APIs.

14

Collaborations with Tech Giants:

AICTE signed Umbrella MoUs with Adobe, Cisco, Microsoft and Salesforce for transforming education through experiential learning. The partnership signifies significant steps towards empowering students, educators, institutions with cutting edge digital tools and resources.

15

MoU with Bajaj Finserv

AICTE signed an MoU with Bajaj Finserv to cater employment opportunities for young graduates in the financial services sector through a Certificate Program in Banking, Finance and Insurance

GLIMPSES OF AICTE ACTIVITIES

16

MoU for Women Empowerment

AICTE signed an MoU with Amazon India to empower and equip women students enrolled in engineering colleges across India with essential skills to thrive in the technology industry.

17

MoU for Students with Disabilities

Youth4Jobs and AICTE joined hands to provide training and placement support to students with disabilities. The collaboration will focus on creating disability awareness among the educators, educational institutions, employers and community. It will also provide free of cost job-linked training to students with benchmark disabilities and placement support.

18

Collaboration on AI

AICTE partnered with Jio Institute for a faculty development programme on artificial intelligence (AI) and data science. The partnership aims to upskill and reskill faculty members from AICTE-approved institutions. It will also explore emerging opportunities within the technological landscape.

19

MoU with Microsoft:

In its continued endeavor to empower students to be future ready, AICTE signed a MoU with Microsoft. The collaboration aimed at creating skilling and job readiness for students and educators associated with AICTE and its partner institutions through a wide array of learning paths, technical and role-based certifications and experiences in areas including AI, cloud, data science, data analytics, and security.

20

MoU with IBM:

AICTE indulged in partnership with to onboard affiliated students and faculty to IBM SkillsBuild and provide them access to digital content, experiential learning, and fresh skills enabling them to take on technical careers.

39 ACTION PLAN FOR TECHNICAL EDUCATION IN AMRIT KAAL

- Making India a hub of Technical Education
- Raising the academic status and ranking of universities to that of internationally accepted world-class universities
- Creating World-class universities dedicated to creating and spreading knowledge in a range of disciplines and fields
- Enhancing excellence in research and development, quality teaching and skill development at an international standard
- Creating a confident, progressive, innovative and empathic generation
- Strengthening the bridge Between Academic and the Industry through the Academia-Industry Collaboration

- Competing in the universal knowledge economy with well-equipped facilities
- Training productive human resources and promoting national development
- Creating an appropriate and navigable roadmap to facilitate genuine, academically credible, and enduring improvements in the quality of the higher education at all levels
- Building robust academic infrastructure with qualified and skilled faculty
- Promoting the education of academically gifted and successful students,
- Raising high levels of funding
- Creation of Knowledge economy to further develop public interest
- Attract the most academically able students and the most highly qualified professors and researchers across the world

40. CONCLUSION

Building a Future-Ready India, A Vision, Plan, and Strategy for Technical Education by 2047, is a path-breaking comprehensive blueprint aimed at unlocking India's potential through Technical Education. With the enhancement of Technical Education, India can play a vital role in nation-building and become a hub for innovation, entrepreneurship, and economic development.

The National Education Policy 2020 and the All India Council for Technical Education (AICTE) are the key pillars of this vision. The policy emphasizes the **importance of experiential learning, multidisciplinary education, and the integration of vocational and Technical Education with mainstream education.**

AICTE, on the other hand, is responsible for formulating policies and regulating Technical Education in India. It has been instrumental in promoting innovation, entrepreneurship, and research in Technical Education through various schemes and initiatives.

AICTE is committed to promote holistic, qualitative, inclusive and accessible education in the country to make India a technical hub by 2047. Being a mentor, facilitator and enabler catering to the needs of its diverse stakeholders, AICTE launched its Approval Process Handbook 2024-27 with introduction of amendments and new provisions. The book elaborates on processes for seeking approval from council with a primary focus on quality of education, simplicity in procedures and transparency in implementation. Some of the new and reformative changes introduced in the APH are as follows:

- Provision for Extension of Approval up to 3 years for well-performing Institutions.
- Introduced Off-campus provision for well-performing existing institutions within the jurisdiction of affiliating Universities.
- Undergraduate Programs/Courses in Computer Applications (e.g. BCA) and Management (e.g. BBA/BMS) have been brought under the umbrella of AICTE to ensure coordinated development in technical and management education.
- Provision for employed/ working professionals to upgrade their academic qualification/ skillsets at diploma/degree/postgraduate level through flexible mode (timings).
- Provision of Hibernation for the Institutions looking for upgradation/revamping of the facilities.
- More clarity on the approval process for Open and Distance Learning (ODL)/Online Learning (OL)
- All AICTE-approved Institutions have default approval for Skilling (through Vocational courses) via making effective use of existing infrastructure facilities and human resources.
- Huge emphasis on innovation through the INDOVATION program and by establishing the Institution's Innovation Council (IIC) on their campuses.

The **Make in India** initiative is another key aspect of this vision. It aims to transform India into a global manufacturing hub by promoting the development of a robust manufacturing ecosystem. Technical Education plays a critical role in achieving this objective by creating a skilled workforce that can meet the needs of the industry.

India has the potential to become the educational capital of the world, thanks to its rich cultural heritage, diverse population, and a vast pool of talented and skilled workforce. By leveraging its strengths in Technical Education, India can emerge as a knowledge capital of the world, attracting the best talent and investments from across the globe.

In conclusion, Building a Future-Ready India, A Vision, Plan, and Strategy for Technical Education by 2047, is a comprehensive blueprint for unlocking India's potential through Technical Education. It emphasizes the importance of a multidisciplinary approach to education, experiential learning, and the integration of vocational and Technical Education with mainstream education. The National Education Policy 2020 and AICTE are the key enablers of this vision, while the Make in India initiative provides the impetus for economic growth and development. India has the potential to become the educational and knowledge capital of the world, and Technical Education can play a crucial role in achieving this objective.